"Just finished reading The 7th Cross. I had a hard time putting it down once I started reading it. I felt like I was one of the characters. I'm intrigued with how you wrote it. It was great to read a book of this nature without all the gratuitous sex and violence associated with this genre. Can't wait for book two!" ~Melanie B.

"I loved how the characters were so intertwined, even though I didn't like some of them very much! No blood and guts and yet the book features a serial killer! Well done! Where's part two?" ~Jeanne B.

"Intriguing storyline with ample twists, turns, and surprises. Likeable characters with not so likeable proclivities. A new crime writer with a redemptive theme." ~Carol S.

"I loved reading this book! I could hardly put it down. It made me feel like I was part of the characters, as it stirred my emotions on more than one occasion. I am looking forward to the next books in this series! Keep up the great writing!" ~Viola A.

THE 7TH CROSS

DD ANDER

www.ddander.com

ISBN: 978-0-9953193-5-6

CONTENTS

JASON

The plan he had so meticulously worked on these past few years was about to be put in play. All he had to do was wait until they once again fell into a drunken stupor, cigarettes dangling from fingertips as usual, and arrange for the still smouldering ember to drop on to the blankets conveniently strewn about. Nothing unusual about that as they spent most of their time laying about anyway. Nothing that should arouse any suspicion.

He hated the monster he was forced to call dad. Jason's rage continued to grow until the age of sixteen when he could take it no longer. He had come to realize that his "memories" were indeed real and now someone was going to pay! As for his mom? God, how he had loved her! And then, how he had come to hate her! How could she have abandoned her own son? How could she become as worthless as him?

She, who had protected him against the drunken tyrant became equally abusive. She had cracked under the strain and now joined him in his nightly drinking binges, and soon the mother who had loved her son more than life itself, was to be found no more.

He made sure they were both sleeping and ever so gently bumped his mom's hand. He ensured that the ember had indeed caught and silently slipped out the back door into the darkness of the night. Making sure he was undetected was paramount and soon he was a few blocks away, perched on the hilltop of the park he had often escaped to, to avoid the hell that he was forced to live in.

Then he saw it, a few flames at first, and then the night lit up before his very eyes. He could hear frantic voices, and a siren screaming in the distance, and still he stayed and watched. From his vantage point he could see everything. The police had arrived, and then the fire truck, and more and more people could be seen scurrying about.

And then he breathed a sigh of relief for suddenly the house became one giant flame, and he knew in his heart of hearts that it was done! Finally!

FLASHBACK

He'd grown up in Portland, Oregon and had a pretty normal childhood, as far as he could recollect. Except he hadn't, not in the slightest. It's amazing how well we can bury or suppress thoughts that would render us completely inoperable. And in some cases irreparable. And that's what happened here. He just didn't know it yet.

How could he know? Secrets were the thing that kept his family together. And isolated from most of the world. No one ever talked about the yesterday's in this family. Today and forward, yesterday is done. Except it would never be done!

So that was his legacy even from a child. Anything he's seen or heard were merely thoughts in his head, or dreams, or in that home, mostly nightmares.

But they weren't mere thoughts. Any horrid nightmares he had were born out of truth. His father was indeed a monster. And he'd conveniently married Rosa, an immigrant from Guatemala, to give his life a semblance of normalcy. He'd wined and dined her but the reality was that he wanted a mate and she wanted to stay in the US. She tried her best to love him. She knew she'd have to make sacrifices, and that she was prepared for, but she knew she could learn to love him given enough time. But soon after their marriage, he began to change.

Change? Not likely. It's impossible to hide reality forever and soon she realized that she had made a deal with the devil. Still she stayed. She excused his absences as best she could, and his drinking. After all, she reasoned, he was under a lot of stress. His business was failing and he had began taking it out on her. Like her previous husband.

Perhaps a child would settle him down. So the morning that she announced that they were expecting a child, instead of reacting to the happy news as she thought he would, he hit her. "How dare you!" he screamed. And the abuse that had come before would pale in comparison to what was to come. "Get rid of it!" But she wouldn't. She would love this child and the child would love her. They would have each other! Who needs him!

But of course, that wasn't true. She did need him, and he needed her. Dysfunction needs companionship and soon these two became as one. But then Jason came into their life, and for a few years she was happy. As happy as she could be given the circumstances. His dad, on the other hand, treated him worse than a dog, and Jason soon learned to avoid him most of the time. But when he couldn't, he was ensured of a beating, whether he had done anything wrong or not.

BACK TO THE PRESENT

But Jason knew he'd have to play their game. So he headed towards home, and when they noticed him approaching he went into his act. "That's my house. Where's my mom? Is she ok?" He screamed! "Mom. Dad!" But there was no answer. He tried to break through the wall of people but to no avail. They held him until the paramedics were able to calm him down. But even then he tried to break free until finally he collapsed and passed out.

The fire could not be contained. No one who had been in that house would survive. And in the light of day nothing remained except for a few objects strewn about.

Of course they questioned him about his whereabouts that evening. But that wasn't terribly difficult to explain, after all, he was a teenager out doing teenager things. They didn't pursue it much further as it was pretty obvious given the strewn bottles lying about. After some enquiries around the neighbourhood to confirm some of the rumours floating about, the fire was ruled an accident, likely caused by an errant cigarette. And that was that.

Everyone knew the parents were drunks and that the son was a bit unusual but he'd never caused anyone any problems. "Poor kid! What's going to happen to him?"

And so he was virtually left alone. Except now social services was involved. It seemed there were no relatives of any sort that could take him in. But he was a good kid, and despite his loss, he seemed to be handling the situation incredibly well.

If only they knew how well he was handling everything! He was euphoric! And just when it seemed it couldn't get any better, more good news came his way.

It seems that despite the pathetic creatures that they were, his parents had long ago taken out a life insurance policy that they had continued to keep active! And now that both of them were deceased, he was the obvious beneficiary.

"There is a God!" He blurted out, but suddenly realized what he'd said. And ever so slowly, his knees buckled and he sank to the cold, hard floor. And he began to sob, and then wail.

They found him that way, and they comforted him as best they could. Poor boy, losing his parents like that. How tragic.

His inheritance was substantial, and fortunately controlled by an executor that had Jason's best interest at heart. Funds were readily available for him to continue his schooling without fear of financial hardship.

To everyone's great surprise, Jason began to excel at high school, and soon he was on the honour roll and fast tracking towards his eventual admittance to Seattle University. He took full advantage of that fact and excelled even more at university than he had at high school. In fact, there were a whole lot less restrictions, and as long as one played the game properly, a degree was pretty much assured.

He'd been drawn to the field of psychiatry his entire life so it was logical for him to enrol in the Faculty of Science, with a major in Psychology which would ultimately result in a Doctorate. Needless to say, he excelled. After all, with the family he had come from, it was a given!

Despite his unfortunate circumstances, he had become the poster child of turning tragedy into triumph. Maybe he didn't have many friends, but who needed them? He had his computer and there was a whole wide world out there just waiting for him.

But beneath the veneer lay the truth. And the truth was ugly. How his mother could have turned on him like that he could not understand. He loved her! He worshipped her! She was so beautiful and she had loved him so much. And then she didn't.

"I hate you! I'm sorry, I'm sorry Mommy . . . I love you mommy." And this is how it would go, night after night. And each morning he would wake up at the foot of the bed curled up in a fetal position, clothes ringing with sweat, exhausted from another night of getting too little sleep. Days became weeks, and weeks became months, and the anger and resentment continued to grow. The strain began to take its toll and his marks began to slip and though he would still graduate top of his class, he was no longer in control of the demons lurking inside his brain.

THE FIRST KILL

That would lead to his first kill. He knew as soon as he saw her that she was the one. At first glance he was taken aback. "Mommy!" Under his breath, thank God, and then he realized how foolish that was. She was the spitting image and as beautiful as he remembered his mom to be. He instantly loved her . . . and then he hated her! Had he possessed a weapon at that moment, she would have surely died then and there.

But now he knew what must be done. It had to be done methodically, like the last one. He could do this and no one would ever know it was him! He'd noticed her name when she'd swiped her card at the dispensary, and made a mental note of it. If she was like everyone else, she'd be easy to find. And she was. FB would be all he'd need to know more about her than she knew about herself! People are so stupid these days! She deserved to die!

Now it was time for him to put his plan into motion. Part of him wished he could tell her to get everything in order to make it easier on the survivors. Why aren't people more organized? His cupboards were more organized than most people's lives!

Jason knew he had to be meticulous. There could be no connection between the two of them. None. He'd followed her the last few days and had finally determined where the murder would take place. People are so predictable! But that was a good thing, and two evenings from now, he would execute his plan. He'd even brought her a gift for the special occasion. It was a simple cross much like his Mom had worn. He remembered how she would caress it as she talked to him about God, and tell him how much God loved him, and how much she loved him. My boy! And he began to cry, and again as he had every night for years, he curled up in a fetal position and finally fell asleep at the foot of the bed.

He could barely contain his excitement as the sun began to set that evening. Soon she'd come down this path as she'd done every night for the past week, alone and oblivious to her surroundings. What was wrong with people? Didn't they know that there were predators everywhere?

And then he saw her slowly strolling his way. He slipped his gloves on, zippered up his jacket, pulled his hood over his head, and waited. If he did this right, one quick snap of the neck is all it should take.

But it didn't quite work out that way. She glanced up at the last moment and as he lunged for her, she side stepped him and screamed. He panicked but quickly regained his composure, and with a final lunge he brought her down, and with a quick flick of his wrists, he heard her neck snap and soon she moved no more. Apparently no one had heard her scream so he stayed with her a bit longer, softly stroking her long auburn hair. "I love you Mommy. Why didn't you love me?" And with that he placed the tiny cross in her hands, stroked her hair one last time, and departed into the night.

When he was safely back in the confines of his home, he broke down. He sobbed without ceasing for hours. Thank God he had made his way home before the floodgates opened. But by morning, any guilt, if that's what it was, was completely gone. And now there were four crosses left.

Jason had long ago given up trying to categorize himself. After his parents' death, he began an intensive study into the supposed minds of psychopaths, and sociopaths, as well as any other path he could think of. The best he could come up with was that he could be deemed a sociopath with psychopathic tendencies. Whatever! They could call him whatever they wanted but there was no way on God's green earth that they would ever catch him!

Still, he wondered why taking a life had virtually no effect on him. Even when he read about the young lady found murdered on the running trails the previous evening, it meant nothing to him. He felt a little sad that she had left behind a husband and two children, but she should have been more careful.

JANICE'S STORY

Janice had never thought of herself as the aggressive sort but here she was asking this guy out on a date! His name was Jason and he had to be the shyest and most awkward guy she'd ever met. But he was also mysterious and incredibly good looking! And that was irresistible.

They had met at a lecture at the University over a month ago, and during a break they had ended up sharing a table at the bistro next door that they had both escaped to. Small talk prevailed as it usually does, and both returned to the lecture together, but alone.

But when the lecture ended, they found themselves once again making small talk which finally led to another trip to the bistro. God, he was quiet! But she persisted and for a brief moment she could have swore that he actually smiled!

He is alive! She couldn't help but giggle at the absurdity of it. She was usually beating guys off, and this guy was barely giving her a glance. As the night drew to a close she managed to squeeze a telephone number out of him, and texted hers immediately to him so that she was at least in his contacts.

Expecting a call or text from him was unlikely but she wasn't about to give up that easily.

And that's how it went. She waited. Three days she waited and no text, no call, nothing. So she texted him. And he responded immediately. Once again, life at the other end!

Since he wouldn't ask her, she asked him to meet her for coffee if he had time. He did, and they met. Three times over the new two weeks, and each time she had to be the initiator. Yet, she knew he liked her. He always accepted her invitations but why wouldn't he call her?

She had to admit that she was definitely the social butterfly of the two. Her gregarious nature was like a magnet and that attracted a lot of attention, not all of it good. Every guy that thought he was God's gift to women hit on her. And by necessity she became incredibly adept at putting them in their place without damaging their all too fragile ego.

But this guy, Jason, must have left his ego at home. Not only didn't he have a line, he barely talked. And man, was that irresistible!

So finally she just asked him out. On a real date. Seriously. And that's all it took. Nothing too heavy, dinner and a movie would be a great ice breaker, followed up by an evening drink at the local pub down the street. God she liked this guy, and he seemed to really like her as well.

From then on, they were practically inseparable. And he talked! He actually talked and he began to tell her about his life. She was horrified and proved to be equally adept at listening as she was at talking. The more comfortable he became the more he opened up. And the more she began to care, and soon she knew she was hooked. Oh my God, I think I'm in love with this guy!

But she had something to tell him, right now. She should have earlier, but this relationship had taken off like a rocket. So she told him about her daughter. She watched him closely as she lead him further into her world. He seemed nonchalant about what she was saying, so she proceeded to tell him the whole story.

She was the usual defiant teenager who knew everything, except that she didn't. Suddenly she found herself pregnant and life was about to take a dramatic turn. That's when she began to understand her parents at a whole different level. She knew that they loved her, even though they were a little pushy on forcing her to go to church all the time, it seemed. She loved going, and was an active participant, especially with the music ministry. But she had an active social life outside the church, and that had finally caught up to her. And now she had to tell her parents.

She recalled that meeting in 1993 as if it were yesterday, not 18 years ago, when she was only 17 and thought the world was her oyster. She had asked then to please come into the living room. That was enough to make any parent nervous but these weren't just any parents. So with tears streaming down her face, and her mother already weeping and her dad looking stoically on, she told them that they were going to be grand parents. And then she burst out crying, barely catching her breath between sobs, so afraid of what might come next.

She should have known, but she was wrapped up in a rather small bundle at the time, and the only thing she felt was condemnation for herself, and she wouldn't blame them if they felt exactly the same. But they didn't. They wrapped their arms around her and they all cried together for what seemed an eternity.

"Honey, we love you, and we'll love this baby just as much!" And that's how Joline entered this world! But there are always consequences for the choices we make. Janice's parents would be there for her journey into parenthood, and they would help her set up her own suite, even if that suite was in the basement of their home. She needed space for her and the baby, and they'd need space as well. They knew they had to handle this correctly; be there for her, but at the same time, not be enablers. Easier said than done. If they could have, especially Janise's mom, they would have given her the keys to the kingdom right then and there!

This was a couple that knew their Lord, and they knew that despite the way this all went down, God had a special purpose for this child and they fully intended on being involved.

Janice had graduated a month after Joline came into this world but any plans of attending university that fall just weren't going to happen. So instead, she enrolled in some online journalism classes which only required a few sessions at the University. This turned out to be a win win situation for Janice as she was able to stay home most of the time to care for her child, but allowed some social interaction at the same time. Of course, her mom was the perfect sitter, and when she was busy, her dad stepped up and did the best that he could. She should have known all along what incredible parents that she had, and she probably did, but this would shape her path over the years to follow.

JASON MEETS THE PARENTS

Her parents were finally allowed to meet Jason. She had talked to them at length about him and how different he was from anybody she had even considered dating. He was so polite, caring, attentive, and an absolute gentleman. What a change!

Janice was not one to hold much back. She liked honest people. Unassuming people. She did not need everyone to like her. She had her opinions and she wanted others to have theirs. There was nothing wrong with agreeing to disagree on any given subject, in fact, it usually made the discussion that much more interesting!

Everything was fair game. She was not one to sidestep politics or religion or any other taboo subject. Bring it on! That's the kind of people that interested her!

And of course, Jason. Obviously intelligent, not arrogant, but very self assured, and quite decidedly his own person. She salivated just thinking about the discussions they had already had and what was yet to come.

When the doorbell rang, it startled her momentarily. "Oh my God, he's here already! How do I look? I'm acting like a school girl! Not a 35 year old woman!" And she giggled! A quick ruffle of her hair and she darted for the door, narrowly beating her Dad. She wanted to make a proper introduction and not have her Dad intimidate Jason before he even got in the house. Her Dad was a large man and liked to come off menacing to her dates. This is my little girl! Don't you dare mess around with her! But he was actually a teddy bear; a big, soft, cuddly teddy bear but they didn't need to know that!

By the end of the evening Jason was a star in her Dad's eye. She wasn't certain, but it was darn near a bromance from what she could tell! There was no doubt that this was going the distance.

Jason knew that Janice loved attending church, and that she led a small study group on Wednesday evenings as well. She was always sharing some new revelation or another with him. He longed to have the faith she had, but he knew he didn't. He talked to God alright, sometimes pleading and sometimes raging at this God who had given him such awful parents. He knew better than to blame God, but He was an easy target and Jason's anger was not easily defused.

But he knew how to play the game. She would never know what he really thought. He'd be there for her, and even attended some of the study sessions whenever he couldn't come with an adequate excuse to miss the meetings. Usually that was no problem as he was often working on projects at the University.

It wasn't that he didn't know God. He did. His Mom had made sure of that. But then she changed and he couldn't understand how an all knowing God could let that happen. He was confused and this would remain with him throughout his life.

Janice led him by the hand through the social jungle until he was as much at ease with her as she was with him. Never had he felt this way! Emotions long buried, swam to the surface, and for the first time in a very long time, he was happy! Within a short time, he was in love and he was pretty sure she was as well!

Time would pass and these two became inseparable. Play had once again become part of his vocabulary. Play, fun, happy, joy, peace, love! Words that were foreign to his life were now front and centre. All because of Janice.

Jason had never even considered being in a relationship with anyone. It hadn't even crossed his mind. When he stopped to think about it, that was strange. Why wouldn't he be involved with somebody? After all, he wasn't a bad looking guy, in fact, according to Janice, he was ruggedly good looking. He smiled as he checked out his reflection in the nearest window and then hurriedly glanced around to make sure no one saw him.

She wondered why he was reluctant to share his past but felt it best to leave that up to him. When it was time she was sure he'd let her in. After all, whatever had taken place in his past, made him the person he was today. And what a person he was! She knew she was in love, and damn it, he'd better be in love too!

He was! In spades! And soon he asked her to marry him. He had just blurted it out! That's not what he had meant to do. He'd rehearsed exactly what he'd say for days. And then in a manner of minutes, he blew it. He couldn't help himself!

It happened so quickly. He'd picked out a ring that he was positive she'd love, and was headed to the restaurant they were to meet at in an hour, so he could get the maitre'd to bring it to the table in the guise of an appetizer.

But as he hurried around the corner of the building, they literally bumped into each other, and without thinking, he dropped to one knee, pulled the ring out of the box, and proposed to her right on the spot! People stopped and clapped, cell phones snapped away, and Janice, ever so graciously, slipped the ring onto her finger, and flung her arms around his neck, and need I say . . . accepted his proposal. She knew him. He was way too methodical to ever do it this way, and yet he had acted impulsively. And that was a very good thing in her estimation. Finally he was loosening up!

Slowly he began to share his past with her. He alluded to the abuse he had suffered at the hands of his dad, and he effused over the love of his mom. And he shared his grief over the death of his parents lost so tragically in a house fire and how he sometimes wished he would have died with them. She held him close as he delved ever deeper into a past that showed little pity for a lost little boy forced to become a man before his time.

He cried as he told her his story. Real tears. But he knew he dare not share too much. They had their own life now and it was good.

She too was an only child, born and bred in this very city. Her parents had adopted a child a couple of years older than she, but she was no longer a part of their lives. Her choice, certainly not theirs. And not up for discussion! Her parents were elated that she had fallen in love with such an incredible man. When he asked for her hand in marriage, they were quick to extend their blessings and offer up their home for the ceremony.

It was a simple wedding, performed in her parents home. There were but a dozen guests, as was their request, and a pastor well known to the family.

They returned to their jobs two days hence, most of their colleagues unaware that anything had changed. And though more outgoing than her husband, she saw no need to share her personal life. And that's how they lived their lives.

THE HONEYMOON

They had married January 3rd but decided to delay their honeymoon until late February so they could escape the bitter cold that the west coast was promising. Playa Del Carmen would be the perfect getaway for our lovebirds. Two weeks of sand and surf, so long overdue, were finally here!

And off they went. He was beyond himself. Never in his wildest imagination had he imaged he could have this kind of life. This kind of woman by his side! He was blessed indeed. Funny. He'd managed to stay single for 35 years and suddenly he was married!

They partied into the night, they slept in as they wanted. They took the bus tour to Chichen Iza, and swam in the cenotes. Fifth avenue tempted them night after night. They were definitely in paradise! And finally with but one night remaining, they made their way to Cozumel, the island paradise just off shore from Playa Del Carmen. And that's when everything changed.

"Mommy?" No God, No. Please. But it was too late. As they boarded the ferry for the return trip back to Playa, their eyes met, she looked away but he couldn't. Janice was a few steps behind and noticed nothing. But when she caught up to Jason, she noticed he seemed distraught.

"What's wrong, hon?"

"Nothing. I must have ate something bad. I'll be fine." He remained silent on the journey, but when they reached shore, he asked Janice to go back to the hotel without him. He'd catch up later. Please!

"Why? I want to stay with you."

"Please honey. There's something I have to do."

"But . . . "

"I'll explain later. I have to go." And with that, he rushed off, leaving her standing alone and confused. What had just happened?

Jason knew that he had really screwed up this time. How the hell was he going to explain this? But he had something to do first. He'd figure the rest out later.

Had he made his first mistake? Time would tell.

He managed to find her in the crowd. This was bad. There were too many people. Too many cell phones. What the hell was he thinking?

And then he saw her enter the Blue Parrot, a popular nightclub in Playa. He followed her in, sat down at a table and waited. Moments later she emerged behind the counter. Thank God! She worked here. Yes!

The urge to see her had revealed something in him he wasn't used to. He had completely lost control of his normally rigid demeanour and exposed himself, at least to his wife. No one saw him like that! No one! And now Janice had. He had some explaining to do and he'd better figure out how the hell he was going to get out of this one! Crap!

But he knew what he had to do, and against every desire his being screamed out at him to do, he did the impossible. He got up, and with nary a glance in her direction, walked out and into the blinding sunshine so typical of paradise. He felt like he had been punched in the gut but he kept walking. For hours, until he finally had a story he felt would satisfy his wife. Then he went back to the hotel.

"Thank God! You're ok. I was so worried." and with that, she threw her arms around him and held him as tightly as she could. She knew he'd explain himself. She'd give him all the time he needed.

He certainly hadn't expected that kind of a reaction! He didn't deserve her! But he sure as hell wasn't going to let her go, not now, not ever! But he knew he had to tell her something.

"Hon, I'm exhausted. Do you mind if we talk about this in the morning? I'm fine. Please don't worry. Everything's fine." And with that, he undressed as quickly as he could and collapsed on the bed.

She decided that she might as well catch the incredible sunset before it also went to sleep for the night. She poured a glass of wine and made her way out to their deck. What a beautiful place! As dusk slipped into darkness, she quietly slipped back into their room. And that's when she found Jason curled up in a fetal position at the foot of their bed. "What the hell?"

He would indeed have some explaining to do! She had decided to just let it go, but now this? There was something going on and she needed to know what! He had indeed made his first mistake!

She had not planned on spending their final night in paradise, he in the bed and her on the couch! But that's what happened. What should have been their final breakfast in bed turned out to be anything but! He lay there bathed in sweat, labouring as in severe pain, oblivious of her presence.

Alright, enough is enough! And with that, she flung open the drapes and ripped the soaked covers from the bed! Any pity she had for him the previous evening had well run its course. "What's going on?"

"Tell me right now!" For an instant he wanted to choke her. He just wanted her to shut up! But she wouldn't! "Now!"

He'd never seen her like this! He'd had it all worked out the night before. He knew exactly what he should tell her, and now? He needed to think! To collect his thoughts, so he lunged for the bathroom and the retreat of the shower. He knew he only had a few minutes to collect his thoughts. He'd have to come clean, at least partly clean. In his worst nightmare he never expected this to happen.

COMING CLEAN

O k, so he'd come clean. What choice? Well, not completely clean, but enough to satisfy his wife, who wasn't too sure who this man was that she was sharing her life with.

So he began to tell his story. About the mom who had loved him so fiercely, and how much he had loved her. And how she had changed and didn't love him anymore. Then he began to sob, and Janice could not stop herself from cuddling this little boy that her man had become. And still he continued to tell her his story. About the fire and how frightened he had been, and how alone he felt. He loved his mommy and now she was gone! His tears flowed, and as much as she tried to contain herself, her tears soon met his and they held each other, he sobbing uncontrollably, she rocking him back and forth as if a baby.

Still he told her more. He thought he had dealt with his parents loss. This had never happened before but yesterday when they'd come off the ferry, he saw his mom. Of course, he knew it wasn't, but it had caught him completely by surprise, and he had to follow her. He sobbed as he talked, and now he couldn't stop the flow of words. He told her more and more, and then he abruptly jumped up and headed to the bathroom.

She heard him coughing and gagging, and finally he opened the door and joined her once again. "Baby, that's ok. We can talk later. I understand." But no. He needed her to know the rest, and he wanted to tell her now. So he proceeded to tell her about following the lady to the bar and how he had watched her for hours, never daring to approach her. He had never had this happen before. "Please forgive me. I'm so sorry! I didn't know what to tell you. I know it's crazy." And with that he began to sob yet again. She stroked his hair ever so gently, like a mom comforting her child. "Shh, it's ok, everything will be ok." And then he knew it really would be ok. He'd told her more than he'd wanted to, but what choice did he have? This would never happen again!

"What a tangled web we weave . . . when first we practice to deceive . . .

JANICE AFTER THE HONEYMOON

Janice wouldn't admit it to Jason, but she had been shaken to her very core. her rock solid man was anything but, and she wasn't sure how to handle it. Of course, she'd prayed about it, but she wasn't about to share what had just taken place with anyone but God! Guaranteed! Had she been blind this whole time? If so, she had a lot of company. Anyone who ever met Jason fell in love with him immediately, especially her Mom and Dad. This would have to be their secret.

So they returned to their life as if nothing had ever happened. Neither spoke of it, and after a time, it was if it had never taken place. But it had. And both of them knew it.

Soon the busyness of life consumed them as each mounted a concentrated attack on their respective careers. janice, ever the organizer, had prepared several weeks of Opinion Pieces in advance. But now it was time to finish one of the several children's books she was working on. She had the audience but as any writer knows, you must keep your children fed or they'll go elsewhere.

JASON AFTER THE HONEYMOON

Jason, on the other hand, went back to his practice. He worked independently and that's the way he preferred it. He set the schedules. He could control his environment as he saw fit. Secrets don't like to be exposed, and he certainly had his share of secrets! Working alone ensured they stayed that way. Except now he was married!

He'd crossed a line that he couldn't take back. Why did he think he could have a normal life? Within days of being married he'd already exposed himself. Janice was no fool and if he wasn't careful this whole thing would blow up in his face. Sometimes he wished it would so he could put his demons to rest once and for all.

Jason knew he'd barely escaped being exposed while in Playa Del Carmen. And even now, he wasn't sure how much of his story Janice had actually bought. Though he had managed to suppress acting out on his urges while there, he knew they were extremely close to the surface. It wouldn't take much to push him over the edge.

But Jason knew no push would be required. He'd managed to escape Playa but he would have his revenge in the days ahead. He had meetings coming up in San Francisco and he knew he would find his "mother" and she'd pay dearly for her transgressions! It mattered not who she was, only that she was his!

So he made the trip once again to the Bank to visit his safety deposit box. There were but a few items contained therein; a few documents still in his possession from that fateful night so long ago. They were of no importance anymore but he kept them anyway. And the crosses. His Mom had told him about them when he was but a small child. There were seven in total; the one she always wore, and six others which represented her family back in Guatemala. It was her way of keeping her family close by. One each for her Mama and Papa, her two sisters, and her two brothers. Jason lovingly caressed the small cross that he wore (his mom's), as he retrieved the next cross that would soon grace the body of "mommy." They'd be close alright!

Jason knew he was going to a place he had not been before. The previous murder had been a reaction to seeing his "mom" suddenly appear in front of his eyes. He could legitimatize that killing in his own mind. This was different and he knew his descent to hell was assured. This one would be well planned, methodical, and drawn out. This one he would enjoy! That's where Angie would come in. And with that, he got up and went out into the night. His work had brought him to San Francisco once again. And it was an opportunity he would not let pass.

ANGIE

She was an absolute beauty by any measure. And that was part of the problem. Most guys wouldn't even approach her as she was obviously out of their league. So, as many beautiful women can attest to, she spent most evenings with a good book, a glass of wine, and her faithful cat, Cuddles.

But after a time that became boring and soon Angie found herself scouting areas of the city late in the evening; areas which she would never have dared venture even in broad day light. Just how much was she willing to push the envelope to get something more out of her life than this boring, mundane existence that she now shared with her cat?

That's how she met Jason. On the pier. Nearly midnight. Not a place she should have been at any hour of the day, especially alone. And there he stood; he seemed to be smirking at her, and it irritated her.

"What are you staring at?"

"You." There was that smirk again. And then "You shouldn't be here. It's not safe."

Before she realized what she'd said, she blurted out "You'd protect me, wouldn't you?"

And that's exactly what happened.

That lead to a drink, and to a conversation that would last for hours. As the sun began to rise, she realized that she had spent the entire night with this complete stranger, and that she absolutely needed to see him again!

She hurried home with barely enough time to shower, and change, and still make it to school in time to lead her Grade 3 class on the field trip they had planned for this day.

She was an extraordinary teacher, loved by staff and children alike. If only all teachers had her love for life, and for learning, and for everyone around her! What a joy!

But she couldn't get her mind off the stranger on the pier. There was something about him, and even with a day's growth, she couldn't help but notice how handsome he was. And, he seemed interested in her! She had to see him again! Tonight!

So she returned to the pier that evening but he wasn't to be found. Strange. She was positive that he had enjoyed the evening as much as she had. So she waited, and just as she was about to call it a night, she noticed a lone figure walking towards her. Please Lord, let it be him! Funny, after all that conversation, she still didn't know his name.

That's because he had purposely not told her, but, he had mentioned that he was from Seattle. He shouldn't have done that. And now here she was again. He hadn't asked for this. She had come to him; not him to her.

There was no one around as usual. He'd made sure of that. Now it was just the two of them. But when dawn began to signal its appearance, it was time to go. But one of them would remain.

They found her body the next morning. At first they thought she was just sleeping. She looked so peaceful leaning up against the pier . . . and she had a tiny cross dangling from her fingers . . .

Why did she have to come to the pier? Why? The silent scream that came from his lips, though unheard by anyone else, threatened to consume him. "I'm sorry Mommy! Please don't hate me Mommy!"

He awoke at the foot of his bed covered in sweat, knowing full well that he had lost the eternal battle yet again. He remembered nothing, but that was little reassurance. He made his way to the door, opening it a crack to reveal the morning paper that showed up as if my clockwork, each and every morning. With trembling hands, he scanned the headlines. It had barely made the paper; just a brief heading: Elementary teacher found dead under pier. That was it.

JANICE REMINISCES

Ff Joline was a chip off the old block, it certainly wasn't on her mom's side. Where Janice was measured and responsible, albeit not at the age of seventeen, Joline was a free spirit. That bothered Janice in no small measure as Joline's dad could be classified thus, back then, and still today. He had chosen not to be involved in Joline's life, in fact, his parents didn't even know they had a grandchild. How sad for them, thought Janice.

But even at her tender age when she bore Joline, she had been responsible enough to ensure that she had her then boyfriend's medical history just in case the future proved unkind. Fine if he didn't want to be part of their daughter's life! But, if, or when I ever need you to step forward, you'd better be there!

She knew how she would have been in a similar circumstance. Absolutely nothing would have stopped her from finding her birth parent. Perhaps Joline wouldn't care, but she doubted it.

Fortunately Janice's parents didn't probe too deeply, and agreed to back off and let her handle it her way. She was pretty sure they didn't agree with her decision, after all, the father bore as much responsibility as she, but they went along with her decision. When she thought back to those formative years, she marvelled at the parents that she had once taken for granted. What incredible people they were. Thank you God for allowing me to be a part of such a wonderful family!

But there was always that feeling of guilt that she felt when she began to reminisce. Guilt over the sister that had chosen to walk away from the family some eighteen years ago. Oh, there had been a few letters on occasion; Christmas, Easter, Mom and Dads's birthdays, for the first few years, and then nothing. As though she or the family were dead.

She remembered vividly when her mom and dad told Janice that she was going to have a sister, and the sister was just a couple of years older than her. Janice was ten at the time, and to have a twelve year old sister was a dream come true! But that dream lasted but six years, and then she was gone! It nearly killed all three of them. How does one walk away from the people who loved you so much?

Her parents tried their best to explain to Janice what had happened, but it rang hollow, at best. The truth was, they just didn't know. She had seemed so happy here! But the truth lie somewhere in the early years of this child's life; the life she led prior to be adopted into their family. This was the past they were never privy to. It nearly killed her parents, truth be known, and it severely altered Janice's perception of the world. Why God? Why?

She had tried in vain to contact her sister but it was if she had disappeared off the face of the earth. And finally, Janice just gave up. But her parents were never the same, and she found that unforgivable!

But as her thoughts returned to Joline she couldn't contain the smile that involuntarily spread across her face. What a character she was! Outgoing, bubbly, an absolute delight to be around! Tons of friends, kind of what she was like when she was her age, that is, until she became pregnant and everything changed. Please God, don't let Joline follow my path!

JOLINE

But Joline had her own ideas. And especially now that her mom was all giddy over Jason. My God, her mom was asking her for advice! What a reversal of roles. Yes mom, good idea. No mom, don't you dare! Too funny!

Since her mom was so distracted and probably going to marry this guy, this was the perfect time to let her mom know what her plans were. She knew her mom wouldn't like them one bit but if there was ever a perfect time to lay it on her, it was now.

"Mom, we have to talk."

"Oh my God! You're not pregnant, are you?" As Janice slowly sunk into the couch.

"Mom! No, I'm not pregnant!"

"Thank God! What a relief, I thought . . . Oh my God, I don't know what I thought."

"Ok, mom, can we talk now?"

"Of course, dear." After that, nothing Joline could throw at her could be that bad, could it?

"Mom, you know I'm heading to University in the fall."

So far, so good, mused Janice.

"Yes, I knew that."

"And I'll be there for the first year, and then . . ."

"First year? I thought it was a four year program."

Here it comes. "It is, but I've been admitted to several study abroad programs. And one of them involves a semester at sea as well. I still get the same degree but in a different way."

"What? You've already been accepted? You never even asked me what I thought?" Janice was beside herself. How could she go behind her back like that. I never raised her that way! And then for a brief moment she realized that she had indeed. She had taught her to be a strong, independent young lady who could hold her own in this male dominated world. Oops!!!

"I'm sorry! You caught me by surprise. Go on, please."

And Joline did. On and on, and on some more. As Janice watched her daughter's excitement she could no longer contain herself and soon found herself transported along with Joline onto the deck of a tall ship racing towards . . . who knows where . . . anywhere . . . and she wrapped her arms around her daughter and they hugged and laughed and cried until they collapsed exhausted. But, oh so alive!

Although Joline had become her own person and made her own decisions, her Mom's opinion mattered greatly to her. She knew when she confronted her about the studies abroad that her Mom would react the way she had, but it surprised her how quickly her Mom had got on board. That was unexpected. But, then again, her Mom was on her own adventure of sorts as well. With Jason coming into her Mom's life everything was about to change, big time!

Joline felt like the adult in their "new" relationship. Having her Mom ask her for advice on relationships was weird. But, she reasoned, her Mom knew she wasn't just her little girl anymore, but a fully grown woman ready to conquer the world. Ok, maybe not the world, but ready to at least push boundaries. And the thought of her Mom vicariously sharing her life with her was a real rush! Maybe other's would think that kind of weird but Joline was over the moon!

Her Mom had taught her a lot over the years. With her words, of course, but mainly with her actions. She had found out she was pregnant at 17 with a boyfriend that was no where to be found. But she was determined that she would raise this child on her own whatever it took. That's my Mom! And what could she say about her Grandparents? They had stood by her Mom and loved her where she was, without judgment. Her Mom often spoke of them and how they had helped her through a most difficult time, but how they had refused to enable her. True love. Non judgmental. Real Christian love, right from the heart. And they encouraged her Mom to take classes and move forward. They'd babysit on occasion but they made it clear that she had made choices that put her in this position and that there are always consequences to our choices. But again, without judgment, simply stating the facts.

Joline knew she'd have to spend more time with granny and gramps in the next while before she went off on her great adventure. They were getting older but were still in excellent health so she'd better enjoy them as long as she could.

Of course, being the only grandchild, and a girl at that, she captured both their hearts, but especially Grampy's. And did he try to spoil her! And did Grammy ever give it to him! But secretly, she wanted to do the same thing. Yet both knew that they would have a huge influence in their granddaughter's life so it was critical that they follow their own rules. So, instead of showing their love through constantly buying her things, they spent time with her doing stuff, and going places. The Zoo became a favourite place to hang out for a few hours, or the park. Her grandparents were unusual to say the least. How often does one see an older couple throwing around a frisbee? That's what they did. And they swam, and biked, and get this, wake boarded. As a result, her Mom, and now she as well, were constantly on the go.

Truth be known, she'd talked to them about her plans even before she broke the news to her Mom. Of course, they were concerned, but she could see the excitement in their eyes. "If you need any help talking to your Mom . . . " but she didn't. She had to do that on her own and she would, but it sure didn't hurt to have them on her side!

And that's how it went. The first year was non eventful as she was able to live at home. Even so, she made a conscious effort to spent as much time as she could with these incredible people in her life. It saddened her when she heard some of her friends talk about their "awful" families and how they couldn't wait to be on their own. I mean, Joline wanted to be on her own as well, but not for that reason. She just knew there was a great big world out there and she wanted to be part of it, not to escape from her family! How sad, and yet how prevalent in our society. Why God? Why is everyone so unhappy?

The next three years were a whirlwind for Joline. She loved every minute of it. There were trying times, mind you. Being caught out in the Atlantic on a tall ship in the middle of a fall storm is anything but fun! But the stories one could tell! She had learned when talking to her Mom or grandparents to tone it down a little. The last thing any of them wanted to hear was "I nearly died last night," or "that was a really close call." A friend's dad had taken her friend aside one night and let her know in no uncertain terms that she best not do that. "Don't you know that your Mom's worried about you all the time anyway? And then you tell her "we nearly died." Got it? Yep. And now Joline got it as well.

She hadn't been home much these past three years and that bothered her a bit. Granny and Gramps weren't getting any younger but they were the first to assure her that "we are quite fine, thank you very much," now get on out of here! "God, I love them!"

She'd made it home to stand up for her Mom when she and Jason married. And, she was the "unofficial" photographer. Her Mom was convinced that her little girl had no equal when it came to photography! Thanks Mom, but there are a zillion great photographers out there. But, if it made her mom happy, then why not! Besides, her Mom was acting like a giddy teenager. And it made Joline feel less guilty that she was off selfishly following her own dreams. Ok, maybe it wasn't selfish! Still.

She managed to get home a couple of times each year but this last visit had been different. She'd felt it the moment she walked in to her Mom and Jason's place. Kind of like when the curtains have been pulled down a little too far. Actually, more of a feeling of despair.

Jason had opened the door, and they had briefly hugged, when her mom came around the corner. When she saw her mom's face light up with her huge smile, she shook off her initial thoughts, and ran to embrace the person she loved most in this world. "Mommy!" Janice loved it when Joline did that. And they hugged as though they may never let go! What a timeless moment . . . "Come in, God, I've missed you sooooo much." "That's my Mom," Joline thought to herself. I am so blessed!

Needless to say, her grandparents were next on the list, so early the next morning, Joline threw on her runners and jogged over to their place. She used to pass by their place on her morning run anyway, and it became part of the ritual to drop in on them before her final 2 mile jaunt home. They knew she was in town, and as if my clock work, she should be arriving any time. "Yep, there she comes. Get out the orange juice!" That was her grampy alright. She could see him on the veranda waving her home, like he did a hundred times before.

Joline had always known she had special people in his life, and thank God, she had never abused that privilege. These past few years had exposed her to a lot of life that she had no idea even existed. So many of her classmates never wanted to go home, or they had no real home to go to, or their parents had been married multiple times, and they no longer belonged, and on and on and on. She knew she was incredibly blessed and she was never going to take it for granted. Never!

Still, she couldn't shake that initial impression when Jason had opened the door at their home. Call it a gut feeling or whatever but there was something . . .

But soon the time passed, and Joline had to head back to school. At least she got to be with them for a week; better than nothing. Her grandparents hadn't changed a bit since her last time home. If anything, they seemed to be getting younger. Ok, she knew that couldn't happen but they were sure doing something right!

But, her Mom. Something wasn't right. Oh, she was her usual bubbly self around Joline, but Joline had seen a lot these past few years, and if her Mom was trying to put one over her, well, it wasn't working. So she asked her "Mom, is there something wrong?"

" No, of course not. Why would you ask that?"

"I don't know. I just feel that something's wrong. You would tell me, wouldn't you? You're not sick or something, are you?"

"Honey, if there was something wrong, I'd tell you. Why wouldn't I?" Why indeed. To herself "oh my God, is it that obvious?"

"Ok, Mom, but don't hold out on me. That's not fair!"

And it wasn't, but Janice didn't have an answer. Just a feeling. And it wasn't going away. But she wasn't about to burden Joline with a "feeling."

"I think I might be a bit more stressed than usual. I have a deadline fast approaching and I've got a ton to do before then. And I'm thinking about a possible book tour and that's freaking me out, and . . . "

"Oh my God, you're doing a book tour! Wow! I guess you'd be stressed out! I'd be so freaked out . . . I could never do it! If someone told me they hated my book, I'd probably punch them out! Ok, maybe not, but I'm glad it's you and not me. Ok Mom, love you, gotta go!"

Janice breathed a sigh of relief. Whew, that was close. And yet, even if she had wanted to, there was nothing to tell her. But now Janice knew that she wasn't going crazy. Joline had picked up on something, as she had, and from here on she'd be paying a little more attention to what was going on around her.

Joline wasn't buying it. Not one bit! Oh yeah, there may have been something to the book tour freak out, but there was something else, and either her Mom didn't know or she wasn't talking. But she knew damn well that something was amiss.

JASON'S ANGUISH

Financially they were doing well. He saw enough clients to ensure an adequate income but still leave him ample time to pursue other interests, including a wife which had never been part of his plan. He hadn't even considered getting married, and now he was, and he'd made a huge blunder to top it off!

Janice had taken a much longer path than he, but through sheer persistence, had climbed the proverbial ladder that led to her becoming a published author of some note. She was proud of her achievements (not too proud, of course), and the money had began to flow. Macaroni and cheese were no longer staples in their home even though they still occupied hallowed spaces in their shelves.

Neither one of them were big spenders so money would be the least of their problems. "How incredibly blessed we are!" and she would physically pinch herself. "Ouch!"

Jason was incredibly well thought of in his field, and even though he didn't mix socially with his peers all that often, he was constantly sought after as a speaker at many of their functions. He, the shy guy, delivered his speeches eloquently as always, and then seemingly disappeared as the night wore on. The truth is, he wandered. He wandered the streets of whatever city the latest function brought them to. Always searching, but for what, he did not know.

There were three such functions yearly; usually one here, and the others spread out down the western seaboard. He loved this opportunity to escape the confines of his daily life, but he also knew that each time he ventured forth, potential trouble loomed.

The truth is, he often drove between Seattle and Portland anyway. He loved the drive and he could drive there and return and no one would be the wiser. It was only 173 miles, and if one avoided weekends and holidays, it only took about three hours. San Francisco, on the other hand was nearly 700 miles away so that was out of the question. Fortunately, his work took him there a couple of times a year, so it wasn't long until he knew his way around San Francisco nearly as well as Seattle. And that was not a good thing for certain individuals that happened to cross his path at the wrong time.

Jason knew that one day this would all come to an end. He never should have allowed Janice to get so close to him. Not like he tried very hard to push her away! But he knew that even though he fought tooth and claw against the demons that pervaded his thinking on so many occasions, he would ultimately give in yet again. It was inevitable.

He couldn't understand how the God he so professed to love would allow this to happen. "Lord, am I doomed to Hell? I've laid my life at the cross over and over. I've given it all to you, but Lord, I can't seem to stop! Help me please!"

This would repeat itself over and over throughout the years. Jason would feel God's presence, and then he wouldn't.

And he had no one to talk to. How could he have? One word of this to anyone and it would be all over. Which would be good, but what about Janice, and her family? "Lord, let me die!"

DAMN YOU, JASON!

Janice's book was in in the final editing stage and she was elated! This was number 7 in a series dedicated to her daughter. And even though her daughter teased her relentlessly about her "little girl," she knew Joline was incredibly proud of her Mom, the author! Janice giggled at the thought. I'm an author! Me!

She remembered back to the time when Joline was an infant, and how scared she had been. And yet, through the love of her parents and of God himself, she knew she would not only survive, but thrive. She'd worked hard, and the rewards soon overcame the fear and the tears, and she knew she could accomplish anything if she put her mind and heart into it. And now, book 7! And then she did what she always did when she got too high on herself, she pinched herself as hard as she could! "Ouch!" And back to reality she came. "That's going to show! God, that hurt!"

Jason had been an absolute gem these last few weeks, knowing that she had reached that obsessed stage that there was no coming back from until this book was put to bed. In fact, she hadn't really thought about anything else, and that was probably a good thing. Since the "incident" her mind tended to automatically "go there" and that's the last place she wanted to spend any time! My God, that was over three years ago! Get over it woman!

And then she became angry. "Damn you! Damn you! Damn you!"

JASON'S DILEMMA

Jason had went out of his way to be as invisible as possible. Thank God she had her book to work on! He'd had quite enough attention, thank you very much! Just how he was going to win back her trust, he didn't know! Not that he exactly deserved it but he'd better figure out something!

He knew that what he had done was irreversible. And that one day the whole sordid story would come out. Why had he let her get so close? How stupid could he have been!

But maybe it wouldn't. Maybe if he prayed more, asked God to take this cruse away from him, then maybe it would be over. It wouldn't take away what he'd done, but at least he wouldn't hurt anyone else. Please God!

And though he pleaded with God, and meant what he said, he knew there would be consequences for his actions, and all would eventually be revealed. Janice would be devastated. Look how uptight she was over that incident in Playa, and that was nothing compared to everything else he'd done! How could he put her through this!

Perhaps if he were to have an "accident." That would be the end of that, and the chances of him being caught would be nearly nonexistent. He could spare her and deal with God over his sins.

But therein lie the struggle. Jason believed in God. He had given his life to Christ but despite that, he was a murderer. Plain and simple. And he deserved to be punished. Or did he? He would pour over scripture for hours on end. He latched on to Romans 7:15 (I do not understand what I do. For what I want to do I do not, but what I hate I do), as well as 1 Timothy 1:15 (Christ Jesus came into the world to save sinners, of whom I am the worst), as well as numerous other scriptures that soothed his tormented soul. And even though he had not extended grace and mercy to his victims, the God of the Bible was all about grace and mercy.

But there were other scriptures as well that pointed to man's responsibility to the laws of the land and of God, and the consequences herein. Scriptures such as 1 John 3:15 made his blood run cold, and Matthew 26:52 showed him no way of escape. Numerous other scriptures confused him even further.

So he held onto what he could. In his heart of hearts he felt that he had repented, in fact, many times. This "thing" inside him that drove him to kill was something he couldn't control. Surely God would understand that. And so Jason remained a tortured soul throughout his life.

THE AUTHOR

Janice had beaten the odds and became a successful children's author. She should have been on top of the world; not only were her books critically acclaimed, but they were loved by her public, and that was the most important of all. Still, she felt like a failure, not in her writing world, but in her real world.

There'd only been that one incident with Jason but she knew in her heart of hearts that something was not right. He treated her extremely well, he and her dad were darn near buddies, he attended church with her whenever he could, heck, he even volunteered at the church on special occasions. The perfect guy. Obviously it was her. And probably it was nothing. Just the overactive imagination of a writer. In fact, she should probably be celebrating. As a writer, you'd better have an active imagination or you were doomed.

She hadn't wanted to embarrass Jason so she held off seeking out the counsellor at their church. Private or not, stuff always had a tendency to slip out, and the last thing she wanted was anyone to think ill of her husband. Besides, hadn't he explained it to her anyway? Why would she have even doubted him?

So they eventually settled into their new lives together. Two individuals coming together in a shared space. Obviously there'd be a few bumps along the way, they had to expect that. But that was more than a bump and they both knew it. My God, that was nearly three years ago! Let it go!

For the past while Janice had been contemplating beginning a new series of books based around a set of 13 year old identical twin girls and journeying with them through the entirety of their teenage years. The kicker was that both of them were definitely "their own person" despite the physical label they shared. She had researched this extensively, as well as talked to dozens of twins, and was convinced that there were stories galore just waiting to be told. Besides, she was starting to get bored with the Joline stories (sorry, Joline). And since her imagination seemed to be working overtime anyway, she might as well put it to good use.

Janice threw herself into this new project as if possessed, and as a result, her and Jason's supposed problems faded into the background. Besides, he treated her like a princess, much to her friends chagrin as "their" guys were a bunch of Neanderthals!

She continued working on the Joline series as before, but now felt confident enough in herself to tackle the "twin" project head on. Jason even got involved and proved to her just how out of touch he really was with the opposite sex! But it was fun! Like it was when they were first dating and Janice knew she had found her prince! Like that!

The years would fly by for these two. Jason was busy building his career, and she was developing "the twins." That's when Janice realized how much weight her name carried in the literary world she chose to be part of. The books still had to be "good," but doors that had remained closed, if not locked when she first began, were now flung open with the mere mention of her name. What a change!

And what an opportunity to share her beliefs through the power of the written word! Now if she could only get a few million readers . . . silly girl! Seriously, these books could have a huge impact if she played this right; just don't go getting all religious and lose your audience, instead, play up values and see what happens from there.

JANICE AFTER JOLINE'S VISIT

Joline's comments had freaked out Janice big time. She wasn't expecting that. Hopefully she had bought Janice's version. After all, it was true, the book tour was freaking her out.

But it shook her up. If Joline had picked up some vibe, it would confirm, at least a little, that perhaps she wasn't imagining things. But that revelation only made her feel worse. Now what?

She knew one thing, it involved Jason. There was something there but she had no clue what it could possibly be. Perhaps because their relationship was too perfect. Wouldn't that statement make her friends gag. A husband that's too perfect? They don't exist. Exactly! Maybe she'd better start paying a little more attention to his schedule, especially his out of town schedule. Funny, that had never even crossed her mind until now. They had such an open relationship and trust that she had never even given it another thought. But now that Joline had picked up "something" she'd better start paying more attention. "I'm probably just being paranoid." she muttered to herself. "God, he'd be so hurt if he knew what I was thinking. Actually, what am I thinking?" she was in a babbling frame right now, and when this happened, she talked to herself constantly. That's how her best story lines developed, but this was not a story she wanted to write.

Janice poured herself into work with a vengeance. She'd worked too hard and for too many years to get to where she was today to let some silly, probably imagined thoughts take her off course. "Smarten up, Janice!" and with her customary pinch "ouch" she was back on track!

The next few months were an absolute whirlwind. Two book releases, dozens of book signings, fortunately most of them in Seattle, a few further down the coast. All thoughts of anything nefarious were pushed to the back of the bus. Jason was incredibly understanding and she "knew" she had let her imagination take her to some dark place that didn't exist in her reality. Thank God she had come to her senses! (At least that's what she told herself)

DEREK

erek was burned out, simple as that! He'd spent over ten years working on the homicide team in L.A. and had seen the depth of man's inhumanity to his fellow human beings. He'd finally reached a point where he had to walk away to preserve his own humanity but he knew he wouldn't stray far.

When he picked up the novel Cold Case Christianity by James "Jim" Warner Wallace, former homicide detective with the L.A. county, he knew what he had to do. No, he wouldn't be chasing down the disciples killers or anything like that, but he could make a difference in the lives of the families of the "forgotten victims" of yesterday.

He found it particularly interesting that Wallace had emphasized over and over that most Cold Cases were solved with good old detective work, not suddenly solved by DNA overnight as in the movie versions. That's not how it worked. In fact, rarely did it work that way. If it did, there wouldn't be over 200,000 unsolved homicides yet today, and that's just since 1980! And if one thinks about the families and friends affected by each and every homicide the figures are staggering!

Barely a month after reading the book, Derek made the decision to join the Cold Case squad, and that's when he found out a whole lot more. Basement, alone, very little if any help, good luck, go for it. Ouch!

And did he! It was as if new life had been pumped into him. Where many considered this to be a step down, it was anything but to Derek. He had indeed found his calling, and if anything, he'd need to pace himself. It wasn't as if there was anyone at home waiting to make him dinner. At least not yet.

He'd met Claire about a year ago at a conference in Houston and she could have easily threatened his single status if he had pursed it a bit more. God, he had wanted to, but he was, quite frankly, chicken! She seemed to like him as well but the conference had ended before his fear did, and she was long gone. Still, he did have her number . . .

Anyway, back to work. So many cases to choose from. Where to start? But start he did, and before long he was getting results, and getting attention from the big boys upstairs. He had shone a small light into a very dark place and life began to replace death. Despair turned into hope. And a few families were able to move on with their lives. He found it impossible to put a price on his feelings, and instead buried himself even deeper in the lives of the "forgotten."

But then he got the call. From Claire, the lady at the conference. She'd be in town for a couple of days and wondering if he'd be up for a coffee.

"Are you kidding me?" to himself.

"You bet. Let me know where you're staying and we can meet for dinner, if that works for you?"

It did, and two nights later he met her face to face for the first time in over a year. God, did she look good! "Don't screw this up, Derek, he muttered to himself.

They never missed a beat, and before either one realized it, three hours had disappeared. And that's when he realized that he hadn't screwed up one bit! What a conversation! What a woman! Now he knew a whole lot more about her, and she, him, and neither was about to let this pass. Needless to say, they would be meeting the next day, and it was guaranteed that Drake would not be working late that night!

She spoke of her investigative work, and her long hours undercover exposing the ugliness of humanities underbelly, and how she felt she was making a difference in a world gone mad. And he spoke of the same. Two different, yet strangely similar worlds. If only they weren't 2400 miles apart! That was a long drive! But, planes do fly every day, don't they? But even by air it was nearly four hours of flight time plus 2 hours checkin on each end. Basically, it sucked!

But there was something about her. This wasn't over by a long shot!

There's something about this guy! He's not getting off that easy!

And that's how it all began. That's when he realized that she would be perfect digging into some of these cold cases, she being an investigative reporter. And that's when she realized what a gold mine Derek could provide. There had to be a bunch of cases that needed her expertise. What they could accomplish together could be incredible! But, the fact remained, they were a hell of a long way apart.

But the conference soon drew to a close and Claire flew back to Houston. She usually enjoyed going home as it gave her a chance to recharge before the next big assignment that often saw her displaced for weeks, if not months, at a time. But this time it was different. Before she even opened the door to her suite, she was lonely. She was alone and it didn't feel good. Not at all. "It's your fault, Derek." she muttered under her breath. "It's all your fault."

He wasn't in any better frame of mind. Suddenly the basement seemed dank and uninviting. And lonely. Had he really voluntarily picked this place to work?

But having a one person pity party wasn't very exciting so reluctantly he got back to work. And after a few minutes he began to settle in and soon he was back to being himself. Well, mostly. But checking for text messages every few minutes didn't help one bit!

Both settled back into their respective lives but they knew their lives had changed. Each would tackle the demands of their jobs as they always had, but each knew there was something missing, and each knew exactly what that was. Both were workaholics and took pride in being so. Neither was that great at relationships, and a betting person would have picked their careers as the winners in this battle. But they would have been wrong. But how to pull this off was the thing.

He couldn't just up and relocate to Houston at a moments notice. She, on the other hand, roamed around the globe continually, so if they were to be together, or at least within commuting distance, she'd have to make the move. And besides, they barely knew each other. Relax. Take your time. What's the rush? Yep. All practical questions. The kind of questions that any decent reporter, or for that a matter, a detective would ask. But neither wanted to be practical!

So they kept in touch, and on occasion, one or the other would fly to the others home for a few days. Over the next year they commuted until finally they knew they had a decision to make. And make it they did. She would make the big move to Seattle. She would get her own place and they would go from there. She'd managed to sell the idea to her boss, and even though it was slightly out of the way, he didn't want to lose her so they had come to an agreement of sorts.

Derek was over the moon. So was she. And Seattle would be the better for it. And so would the cold cases, and perhaps a few more families would finally get the peace they needed and the perpetrators the punishment they so rightly deserved.

She'd always loved forensic science and as an investigative reporter she was able to access information that would allow her to go down bunny holes few ever had access to. And now that she and Derek were working together, albeit for different organizations, she was granted access to certain files that she definitely couldn't have access to without a whole lot of sucking up. Of course, he benefited as well. Anything she dug up that might prove useful she passed along. And that had helped crack more than one cold case, and made Derek the unofficial poster boy in the Cold Case Division.

He had worked as though possessed while with the homicide division. But it paid off, until the burn out, that is. Case after case was transferred to the solved file. Now the same thing was happening with the cold cases. And having an investigative journalist looking at the cases proved to be a huge advantage!

Interestingly enough, one of the cases he was currently working on seemed to really speak to Claire. There was something about this one . . . so he gave her full access to all his files. If anyone asked, she was doing contract work for him. But this one was different, and soon, she'd know a lot more than she ever wanted to know about that case.

They had started discussing this particular case like they had so many others over a bottle of wine and pizza late one Friday night. They had become close, these two, and she'd even moved to be closer to him, but both were afraid of losing what they already had. Nuts! They acted like a pair of eighteen years olds instead of thirty somethings!

So they talked as they ate and sipped on their wine while he filled her in on the case he had just put aside. Claire had proven herself time and again that she had what it takes to land the big ones. And besides, now that she was here, it meant he could spend more time with her. Definitely a win, win situation.

There would never be enough time in his lifetime to address even a fraction of the cases that he was personally involved in, and there were hundreds of others doing the exact same job he was. How utterly depressing for the families torn apart knowing full well that the person or persons that took their loved ones life may still be out there doing the same thing to others right now. Why he stuck with this job he did not know. Still, with each victory, though they were few, he knew that at least some lives would be saved once the perpetrator was behind bars and the families of the victims would find some degree of peace. At least a little.

CLAIRE AND
O'MALLEY

Derek wasn't happy. Claire had headed to Portland to meet O'Malley, the retired detective who had worked on her brother Mikey's case. Apparently he had some inside info that she had to have. He didn't blame her for going. Hell, I would've done the same. Still, he wanted her here.

He'd never realized how much he'd been missing in his life until she came into his, and now he was all screwed up. Screwed up in a good way.

"I love that woman." To himself, and then glancing around to make sure no one was listening "I LOVE YOU, CLAIRE!"

Then ever so faintly " Then tell her, you idiot!"

Oh my God!

And that's when Greta walked around the corner. Greta, the cleaning lady. "Tell her, not me!" and off she went.

How flipping embarrassing was that! Great! Now the whole world would know. Sure as hell, she'll post it on FB or something, or tell everyone here, or . . .

Or perhaps when Claire gets back, he'll just tell her himself. How about that?"

Good idea, Derek. Good idea.

Having Claire around changed everything about the job. Whenever he'd get stuck on a case, which happened frequently, he'd get her to take a look at it. It didn't always pay off but they'd had tremendous breakthroughs as a result of different eyes looking it over. Often a detectives and a reporters view of the world were pretty similar, but there were still subtle differences, and that could make or break a case. He should know. Several witnesses could be at the same scene of a crime and each one see it differently. That's why witness statements were often notoriously inept. And that's why witness statements were only a small part in the eventual breaking of a case.

Recently there had been several cases that were technically Cold cases, but recent activity had thrust them back into the lime light. Old became new again and lines often became blurred. Just when does one let go a case they'd been working on for so long and turn it over to the new guys? He'd worked homicide previously, and now cold cases, so he fully intended on being involved right to the bitter end.

Derek had garnered a reputation for taking care of business promptly and efficiently, so he was extended courtesies not available to just everyone. Besides, if he wanted to their job for them, why not? And that's where Claire came in. Fresh, non detective eyes and an uncanny ability to see the unseen made her invaluable. He got his man. She got her story.

CLAIRE RETURNS TO DEREK

She wanted to surprise him. He wasn't expecting her until the following day so she called his buddy, Roger, and asked him to arrange a late dinner at their favourite place. Use whatever excuse he had to, but make sure Derek showed up. And then of course, excuse himself, go to the bathroom or something, and then get the heck out of there. Leave the rest to her.

It didn't take long for Roger to "get it." He'd figure out something. But Claire would be owing him big time and she'd better not forget it!

All Derek could think of when Roger asked to meet him at that particular restaurant, which certainly wasn't where they would normally meet, was that Roger must be in some kind of trouble, probably with Shelly again, his on again, off again girlfriend. Like he could offer any advice! If he was on the ball himself, he would have long ago told Claire exactly how he felt. None of this beating around the bush stuff! Oh well, he's a good friend. See you at 8.

So he and Roger met. Roger seemed nervous. Maybe there was a lot more to this than he had thought. Just as they were about to get into it, Roger suddenly excused himself and headed to the bathroom. Crap, is he ever acting weird, thought Derek. Oh well, he'd invited me so I might as well let him tell me in his own way.

He studied the menu, although that was unnecessary. He and Claire had been here a number of times . . . Jeez, I wish she were here . . . He chuckled to himself "Garçon, the young lady would like the . . . ". If only. And that's when he looked up . . . "Claire!"

"Can I sit down or are you just gonna stare?" she was loving this.

"Yes, of course. I thought you weren't back until . . . God, you're beautiful." And she was. She had chosen the dress carefully. Dark red, flowing skirt, plunging neckline, and freshly coiffured hair. And his reaction. Priceless!

"I hope you don't mind if I take Roger's place. Apparently he got called away. Will I do?" Oh yes, she would do fine, thank you very much!

So now Derek knew what to order "Garcon, the young lady would like . . ." but before he could finish, she shewed the waiter away, bent over and kissed Derek passionately, and then returned to her chair as if nothing had even happened. But it had! And then "Derek, I love you, and you'd better love me too, because otherwise I'm going to look like a complete idiot!"

"I do. Oh my God! Yes!" And before he knew it, he'd blurted out what he had been longing to say forever "Will you marry me?" He didn't even have a ring. Of course he didn't have a ring, after all, he was meeting Roger.

"Yes! Yes, my God, Yes!"

As for the ring? Well, they'd pick that out together!

They both wanted this, but neither would make the move, and now in a matter of moments they had committed their lives to the other. As for the food? Who cared!

And then it was back to work for both of them. Claire's boss found her unusually chipper when they spoke the following morning. Claire was usually so acerbic that he always had to be on the ball to ensure he caught what she was really saying. Today? Definitely not the Claire he knew.

"Okay, what's up?"

"Excuse me?"

"Spit it out. What's going on?"

"I don't know what you're talking about. I thought you wanted an update."

"I do but first of all, I want to know what's going on."

My God, was she that obvious? She'd better give him something. I know, I'll tell him about my brother.

"You remember I told you that I was going to dig into my brothers case when I had the time? Well, I went up to see him this past weekend. That's all."

"Do I need to remind you that I'm no fool. I know you Claire, probably better than you know yourself. Now, spit it out!"

He knew her alright. She loved her boss. Go figure. He'd followed his gut and let her fly when others would have preferred that he clip her wings. She'd proven him right and she certainly owed him more than she was giving him right now.

"You're right. There's lots happening up here. I can't wait to tell you, honest. But, could it wait until I'm in Houston on Thursday? I promise, I'll tell you everything!"

He had to chuckle. That's my Claire! "Okay, but you come see me the moment you get here!"

"I promise!" In actuality, she was excited to talk to him. He was one of the few people she could really confide in. But now, it was time for an update!

When Derek got back to the office the first person he went looking for was Greta. When he found her, he grabbed her and started to dance but she was having none of it. "What's got into you? Let go of me!"

"I did it! I did it! I asked Claire to marry me! And she said yes!"

"Lucky girl." She deadpanned. "Now let me go!"

As Derek floated off down the hallway, Greta couldn't help but chuckle to herself. "I guess all he needed was a kick in the butt. But he'd

better not try that again or next time I'll smack him!" to no one in particular.

Derek had a couple of cases that were nearing completion and he was hell bent on putting them to bed. In both cases the perpetrators had been identified and were now under police supervision. It was just a matter of time. Two more families would be able to move on knowing that the killers were finally paying for what they'd done to their family members. Hopefully they would get closure. At least some.

THE LATINO SERIAL KILLER CASE

But the case he was most intrigued by was finally going to get the attention it deserved. And Claire had been drawn to the file as well. She couldn't explain it, but this was one she wanted real bad. And finally, he'd be able to spend the time on it that it deserved. When a current homicide merges with a cold case, there's always room for optimism as it could be the straw that finally breaks the camels back. This homicide had occurred only a few months ago, and even though it remained unsolved, the MO was the same as a half dozen others that had ended up on his desk. The warmer the trail the better chance of resolution.

When he told Claire that they could finally work on a full case together, and particularly on this one, she was beside herself. Put the two of them together, and watch out bad guys. You're going down! Of course, understand that I do have a boss and he expects me to do my job while I'm up here.

She'd flown back to Houston, and exactly as commanded, went to see her boss. He saw her coming before she burst into his office. This was going to be good!

And it was. She told him about Mikey. She told him about some of the cold case files she was working on.

"And?"

"And what?"

"Do you think I was born yesterday?"

And that's when she began to laugh, and cry, and she hugged him unabashedly. "Wow. Where's Claire? Who the hell are you?" And they both began to laugh.

"I'm getting married! Derek and I are getting married! I need you to walk me down the isle! Say you will. Please!"

He'd never, ever seen her like that. Positively giddy. Claire. The Iron Lady. No wonder she wouldn't tell him on the phone. And now she wouldn't stop talking! On and on and on. My God! Usually he couldn't get her to tell him anything without threatening to pull her teeth. Now she wouldn't shut up! So, he let her ramble, and then he let her ramble some more. And finally "Enough already!" And yes, I'll walk you down the isle!" Another quick hug from Claire, and he watched as she practically danced out of the room. "What a woman!"

And then it was back to Seattle. And her future groom! Surreal! She'd been involved a few times over the years but work always came first, and for some reason, men didn't seem to get that. Probably because most of them were just little boys! Besides, they would have complicated her life way to much. And expected her to always "be there" for them! Yuk!

But now, at the age of permanent 39, she was finally ready. Oh my God, was she! Interestingly enough, Derek had never been married either, although he alluded to being in a couple of longer term relationships. So at least that should be in their favour.

It's not like she hadn't thought about this earlier. Just in case. Besides, she was a reporter and reporters like making lists! Let's see: both single; neither had children; both had good, solid careers; both were independent sorts so space shouldn't be a problem; neither smoked or did drugs; they both enjoyed a glass of wine, or a drink on occasion, but no issues there; there didn't appear to be any trust issues or overt jealousy; both were the outdoorsy sorts; and so on. What else? Oh yeah, he was a Christian and she was, not exactly sure, but if she had to coin it she'd call herself agnostic. I mean, she'd went to church with her step parents for several years and had participated in a bunch of church activities. She even remembered giving her life to Jesus during one of the rallies but nothing ever really came of it so I don't know. Agnostic, I guess. Hopefully that wouldn't be a problem. And one more thing: she couldn't remember Derek ever talking about his parents. Odd. She'd better check that out. And the religion thing.

And then there was Derek. He did his man thing. Yep, we're compatible. I love her, she loves me. We can do this! I gotta give her a call right now. So he called, and the first thing she said after the "I love you" stuff was, "we gotta talk." Oh oh!

That's part of the reason he had stayed single so long. Women were downright confusing. Just when you thought everything was going along smoothly, they'd want to talk! And that usually involved a lot more than just talking (same word, different definitions).

He'd wanted to get together to discuss the impending case. She wanted to get together to discuss the two of them. It was pretty obvious which one was going to win, wasn't it?

"I love you, and you love me, right?" so far so good. She continued "And we want to make sure that we are always on the same page, right?" Ok, and "We don't want to have any secrets between us, agreed?" "Agreed." Where was this going? Maybe she knew something about him that he didn't even know about himself. Women are like that!

He'd better start speaking up " where are you going with this? Did I do something wrong?"

"Why would you think that? Did you?"

He shouldn't have said a word. Far better to just let her interrogate him or whatever the heck she was doing. Just answer the questions. If you need a lawyer, ask for one.

She continued "I told you about my family and I shared with you about Mikey, right?"

She had.

"But" He could feel it coming. "You haven't told me a thing about your family. I don't even know if you have one. Do you?"

Finally. "I thought I told you. My parents were killed in an auto accident when I was like, 23, nearly 17 years ago. It was a head on with a semi. They never had a chance. I was the only child. I could have swore that I told you that the first time I met you back in Houston. In fact, I'm sure I did."

Claire could feel the blood draining out of her face. "I'm so sorry. Please forgive me. I feel so dumb!"

"It's okay, it happened a long time ago."

"But I should have remembered that. What was I thinking?"

"Okay, now that we have that cleared up, anything else?"

There was, but Claire wasn't about to screw that up too! Perhaps a different approach. "Hon, have you ever thought about having kids?"

Derek nearly choked on that one. He had to ask "You want kids?" Oh boy!

And then Claire began to laugh. She'd made a list; she'd checked it twice, and yet she had completely forgot to ask about kids!

"No, I could never see myself as a mother." This might be a deal breaker.

"Thank God!" Derek could barely contain himself. "I love kids, other people's kids. Next question please."

Definitely! That was close! "Derek, I know you love going to church, and since I've been in Seattle, I've went with you every time, right?"

"I'm glad you brought that up. I've been talking to Pastor Rick and he wants us to drop in to see him one of these days. They have a marriage seminar they want everyone to take before they'll marry them. It's only a couple of days long. I think it starts on a Friday night, and is over late Saturday. I told him I'd talk to you before we committed to a time. I hope you don't mind me jumping the gun a bit but when I saw him at Wal Mart the other day, I had to tell him the good news! I really like that guy."

"Well, I guess that settles that. Ok, now where I do I go?" Claire muttered to herself.

"Hon you know I'm kind of on the fence a bit when it comes to religion. I told you that, right?"

"I guess" hesitantly, this was getting confusing.

This wasn't going well. Smarten up Claire! She admonished herself.

"Hey that's great. You set it up with Pastor Rick and give me as much notice as you can so I can get the time off. You know my boss! He thinks he's a lot more important than you! Just kidding! By the way, I asked him to stand up for me. I hope that's ok with you. I should have asked you first but he's the closet thing to a dad that I have and I didn't think you'd mind . . . ok, I'll shut up now."

When she got going . . .

But now Derek was confused. They'd never even discussed going to church. They just went. He hadn't really thought all that much about it. He'd been a Christian for, like forever, and even though he'd kind of done his own thing over the years, he still attended church whenever he could. He had to admit, working homicide made it very hard to believe in a loving God! But if he didn't even have that, then what was the point of anything.

Fortunately, he was a reader as well. Factual stuff. Investigative stuff, and when he heard about Wallace's book, his faith was definitely given a kick in the pants. And then he read Lee Strobel's books, the Case for Christ and the other one, The Case for Faith, and that's all he needed. Never questioned after that. Just resolved to be the best person he could be. Besides, he probably wouldn't even be working on cold cases if it weren't for Wallace!

He and Claire were going to have to talk about this a bit more. No matter! He loved her and they'd work it out! At least they both agreed: no kids! Whew!

BACK TO THE CASE

Claire had let her boss know that she and Derek were actively engaged in a cold case that was bumping up against a recent homicide that had the exact MO of the cold case. This was the kind of break investigators dreamed about. And she would have the exclusive! Of course it didn't hurt one bit that she may have been involved just a little bit with one of the lead detectives! That's the breaks!

So they were able to finally put some resources into the case. Claire's gut told her to concentrate on the crosses. Once again, it was exactly the same as the others. This was no coincidence. But now she had carte blanche to pursue it however she chose.

Her online research had given her a few clues but nothing beyond what she had already surmised. It was time to pound on a few doors and the first door she was pounding on was the Centre for Multicultural Education. If anyone could point her in the right direction, it should be these folks.

It was pretty obvious that the cross had to be significant to the perpetrator(s). But, because the victims were from several different countries; Columbia, Honduras, Mexico, Guatemala, and now the US, it didn't seem to make a lot of sense. But at least it was a start. If the cross could be identified even by country, we may have a starting point. Our first victim, as far as we know, was from Honduras. Anything is better than what we have right now.

DEREK BACK TO
THE CASE

While Claire continued to work the cross angle, Derek continued to work on the time line. He knew it wasn't safe to assume anything, but, he had to work with what he had. Six murders for sure, perhaps more, given the large time gaps between some of the murders. Not an ounce of usable DNA from any of them! Still, there were enough similarities that a good eye should be able to detect a pattern. He had an eye for such things and so did Claire. Geez, I wish she had more time to work with me on this!

Turns out she did, he just didn't know it yet. Her boss had cleared her schedule. Of course, he fully expected her to pull off this case, and as he liked to joke, especially since you have inside information. "Claire, you sure do take your work seriously, but even I didn't expect you to marry the guy just to get a lead!" Ha, ha!

And in she walked. "Guess what babe?"

He "Surprise me."

"You're stuck with me now. Full time until we solve this case. Too bad for you."

"Are you serious?"

"Why? You don't want me here? I can always ask my boss for another assignment."

"No, no, no! But seriously?"

"I'm all yours, babe, at least until we wrap this one up!"

"There is a God!" Derek.

"You didn't know that?" Claire.

He knew she knew there was a God. Enough word games. Time to get to work!

THE SUMMARY

As close as Derek could surmise, the perpetrator had begun his reign of terror in Seattle. Or at least, that's what the clues pointed towards. If he was right the first murder took place in Oct/96. The victim was a young Mom, 32 years of age, out jogging when she was attacked. Even that was strange. Another jogger found the young lady propped up along the trail, seemingly just relaxing. He stopped to chat for a moment and that's when he realized something was wrong. He knelt down and that's when her body fell over, scaring the hell out of him. He quickly called 911 and waited for the police to arrive. The autopsy determined that her neck had been snapped. There were no other marks, but, a small cross had been intertwined around her hands, which led officers to believe this might have been personal. But nothing ever came of it. In fact, there were no suspects at all. Ok, other points: she was a US citizen but formerly an immigrant from Honduras. She had two young children. Nothing extraordinary about her life as far as we could tell. No trouble with the law. No nothing. A great marriage, kids, friends, family. She appeared to have it all. And yet here she was. Dead.

Derek continued "It appears our perpetrator got busy once again, this time in Portland in Feb/98, nearly two years after the first one. Again, it was a young lady, 25 years of age, single and sharing an apartment with a friend (girl). Again, no signs of anything amiss. Not overly active on the dating scene. Finishing up her masters at the Univ., and heading towards a solid career in finance with the Washington Federal Savings and Loan Association (where she already worked on a part time basis). She was well liked by everyone who knew her. Again, nothing unusual. By the way, she was a US citizen as well, born and raised here to Columbian parents. They had come here to escape the violence in their country. Ironic, isn't it? Once again, she had been discovered by a passerbyer on his way to work via Jackson Park. He noticed her slouched over on a park bench and thought something was wrong with her, especially when she didn't acknowledge him. So he tapped her on the shoulder, and that's when she slid to the ground. Horrified, he called 911 and then checked for vital signs. But, it became readily apparent that she was already dead. The coroners office once again ruled it a homicide, and as before, cause of death was a broken neck. And once again, there was no struggle. Just a clean kill. And once again, investigators found the young lady's hands clutching a tiny cross."

Derek stopped for a moment to compose himself, studying Claire as he did so. She sat as if enraptured at what she was hearing.

"Oh my God! Was it the same kind of cross as the other woman?"

"Yes. But at the time it didn't really mean anything. So once again, the case eventually became cold and ended up in File 13. You know what I mean." And she did. How sad for those left behind. But she knew Derek wasn't done yet and she wasn't about to stop him now. He was on a roll and she was hungry for more.

"I wish I could say that that was the end of it but I think it was closer to the beginning of his reign than the end of it. The next time he struck, as far as I can tell, was in May/2001, again in San Francisco. That's 3 years later which seems really odd. It's like he was locked away or out of the country. I wouldn't be surprised at either scenario. If he was out of the country there's a great likelihood that there are other victims as well. But, that's all I have dating back that far. By the way this one was Latino as well, from El Salvador. Same MO. Broken neck, a cross woven between her fingers like the others, and once again, propped up to look like she was just resting. Again, someone stopped to see if she was alright and when they touched her she fell over.

"Wow! Three victims at least! But that was a long time ago. Why are you so intrigued by this case?" Claire was confused.

"I'm not finished. There's more. Believe it or not, six years later our same guy showed up again."

"Seriously?"

"Yep. Mar/2007. Same M.O. as before. Young Latino lady, in Grand View Park, San Francisco found strangled to death, and a small cross woven between her fingers just like the others. But now investigators were beginning to draw some parallels. But even then, there was nothing, not even a suspect. This guy was either a professional, which made absolutely no sense, or he must have worked in the medical field in some capacity to leave absolutely no physical evidence." He paused and Claire jumped in.

"Maybe he's just a drifter. But that doesn't make any sense either, does it? There has to be some common denominator besides the cross that ties him to all of these women. Let's see: all women, all of Latino origin, all attractive, all upstanding citizens with no criminal or unsavoury links anywhere, all with crosses woven around their hands. And the crosses were all the same, right?

" Not sure. We'll check that out but there's more."

"You mean there are still more victims?"

"Two more for sure. Probably more, but I can't find any evidence of that. Not yet anyway. The second last one seems to have occurred in Jan/2011. At least, that's when a young lady by the name of Angela ended up exactly as all the others had. Same M.O. exactly. Oh, and it was also in San Francisco. By the way, she was Caucasian."

"That's weird. Are you sure it's the same guy? Was there a cross? Why would he change his MO?" And before he could answer "that makes three in San Francisco. He's got to be from there."

"I don't think so. But the reason I'm telling you all this is because of the last one. Get ready for it. It happened right here!"

"Here? In Seattle? Oh my God!"

He loved it when Claire got excited. Her expressions . . . ok, moving on.

"About three months ago. Same M.O. as the last one. It's like he's come home. Interested?"

"Yes! Oh my God, yes!" And that's when Claire really went to work. The last murder occurred the night of Dec 14/2015. The old cases were butting up to the new and she had full intention of being a witness when this guy was taken down once and for all!

How could someone destroy so many lives! My God, was he just evil or what the hell was going on in his mind? This was something she could sink her teeth into, and like Derek often kidded her, she would never let go!

Of course she mustn't forget that she had a "real job" that needed attending to. She was well aware of the responsibility that had been placed on her and she wasn't about to let anyone down. She had fought long and hard to achieve the success she already had in the crazy world of journalism and she wasn't about to let it go anytime soon!

This cold case wasn't going anywhere, but now that she had permission to fly, she'd be on it like a dog with a bone! And besides, wouldn't her boss be happy that he'd once again made the right decision by letting her relocate to Seattle!

The torrid pace that Claire called normal, finally caught up to her, and suddenly she found herself stuck at home in bed for a week. "Young lady, either you get your butt home and stay there for a week, or I'm going to admit you! Your choice!" "Yes Doctor!" What a grouch! Of course she said that under her breath. No way did she want to be stuck in a hospital! My God! Being stuck at home was bad enough!

But with every downside, there is an upside, and it wouldn't take her long to find it. Ha! I can spend some time on this cold case as well as do some research on my own families case. The one she'd been putting off forever. No more excuses, Claire! The good Doctor and her boss had obviously colluded and she was "relieved" of all duties for at least a week. "Call me when the Doctor says you're cleared and I'll put you back to work." Fine!

So with lots of pouting and some tea and consommé tossed in as side dishes, she set about getting well as quickly as possible. But it would take time and she sure wasn't going to waste it all watching TV!

The further she delved into the file that Derek had so graciously copied for her, the further she became convinced that the cross was the key. Others had reached that same conclusion but hadn't followed any further than noting it in the files. She became convinced that all the crosses on the victims were identical. Sure, each victim bore a cross. Everyone knew that, but no one had seriously looked into tracing the actual cross to see if it could be sourced. After all, there are millions of crosses. This could be mission impossible.

But she was convinced otherwise. These were no five and dime costume jewellery crosses. The design was intricate, exquisite in fact. And that alone convinced her to carry on.

Since she was stuck at home, Google would have to start searching for her. And search it did. Thank God she had learned long ago the power of keywords! It took awhile but finally she found it. Well, not really, but enough info to suggest that this type of cross held special significance for a certain culture. Bingo! Somewhere to start!

CLAIRE

Claire's emergence into a new world began the moment she walked onto the Campus at the University of Houston. She'd been raised in a great home but knew she never really fit in, and was anxious to find her true self. She knew she'd be completely alone here, but that is exactly what she relished. She'd worked her butt off in school, and now with the advantage of several scholarships, she could fly on her own. And fly she would.

The next four years were a dream come true for our girl, and she emerged with a degree in Journalism, and to no one's great surprise, top of her class. Now she was working with a major newspaper and apprenticing as an investigative reporter under an incredible mentor. As if that wasn't enough, she was in the beginning stages of writing a novel (who isn't), as well as blogging on a regular basis. Claire was actively looking for The Story that would let her play with the big boys!

Claire was a loner, and though she had many friends on campus, she was notorious for always wanting to be alone. It frustrated her friends to no end, but she was the type of person who could tell you to take a hike and you'd still enjoy the journey!

She rarely talked of her past, and soon it became obvious that the topic was not up for discussion. Period. But, that didn't mean she didn't think about it, and in fact, it probably led her to pursue the career she had chosen. But, enough psychoanalysis, there was work to be done!

What Claire chose to bury as deeply as possible were the first eleven plus years of her miserable life. She knew full well that when Pandora's box was opened it would be impossible to put the lid back on again. Although she had been rescued, at least physically, from hell itself, psychologically it was quite another matter. Especially when she refused to share her life with the myriad of professionals who poked and probed her like some specimen under glass.

Oh how they tried to rescue her, to bring her back from that dark place. She was placed in a loving home for a number of years but she could not reciprocate the love extended to her. And when she could legally move on, she did so, and rarely looked back.

Looking back now after the passage of some thirty plus years, she knew she had some serious amends to make, and she had some skeletons in her closet that needed to be exorcised once and for all.

She'd seen it all in her career as an investigative reporter, and had in fact, broken several large stories that brought down some very powerful individuals. Claire had been threatened on many such occasions and more than once felt that she may not live a very long life. But as time when on, she became calloused to the multitude of threats that seemed to come and go like the wind, and became zealous in her pursuit of what she considered justice long overdue, particularly for the rich and powerful.

They thought they could buy their way out of anything, and often did, but they soon learned she was not for sale. Not at any price. Thank God she didn't have a family that they could use as leverage against her!

Thank God! Really? Ok, someday I do want my own family. Some day, just not now.

She had begun to open Pandora's box a few years ago, knowing full well that she could never seal it up completely ever again. So she dabbled around the periphery and was finally able to gain access to her entire file. That's what happens when you become a "star" in this world. You gain access to files that you should not be able to. This was one of those files kept under lock and key, and still remained thus, but now she had a copy of it in its' entirety.

Dad, mom, brother, sister. Dad murdered. Mom institutionalized. Brother on death row for murdering his father. Sister sent to an orphanage. That was all back in 1983. Sister adopted in 1986. End of story.

But it wasn't the end, and it certainly wasn't the beginning! Claire had worked many, many cases involving heinous people, and she'd developed a thick skin but this one was different. This was up real close and personal, and she knew full well that you can't "unsee" something once you've seen it. And from what she'd been told by those who had worked the file, it was nasty.

MIKEY

Michael (Mikey) was 15 when he decided that his dad had beat his mom for the last time. And that he needed to protect Claire from what he knew his dad would soon do to her. His dad had even bragged to him that she was almost "ripe" and he'd be the one picking the fruit.

So when he picked up the shotgun and methodically loaded both barrels, he knew there would be no turning back. And he knew he was likely to be executed or die in prison. But at least the world would be rid of that piece of garbage.

When he heard the truck pull into the driveway that Friday night he knew the time was near. If his dad pulled his usual act, he'd come into the house, demand to be fed, even though supper had been served two hours prior when he said he'd be home, and then berate his wife (their mom) for being a useless fat pig. If she dared respond, his fists would do the rest of the talking.

What was so sad was that their mom had suffered a severe mental breakdown and was incapable of taking care of herself, let alone a family, and especially an abusive husband. Any self esteem that she once had was long since gone. She had long ago resigned herself to the fact that this was her life. The kids, well, they had learned how to hide whenever he was around. They loved their mom but she needed to be in an institution, they knew it and their dad knew it, but that cost money, and his booze was a hell of a lot more important than her!

Mikey waited for the usual argument to ensue, and as if on script, he heard the slap and then his mom's blood curdling scream. He took a deep breath, walked into the kitchen with the shotgun levelled at his dad. At first his dad jumped back and then he lunged at Mikey. And that's when he let his dad have it. Both barrels. In the chest. Then he dialled 911.

Claire never saw Mikey again after that night. All she knew was that he had killed her daddy, the daddy that had loved his little girl. At least that's what she thought at the time. And her mom was institutionalized. And she was sent away. And it was all Mikey's fault!

But as she began to peel back the onion she began to notice discrepancies that were impossible to ignore. She had been told that her brother was an "evil" person, probably a psychopath, and she was lucky to still be alive. She was told that her daddy was a good man, and that her mom was very sick, and that may have caused her dad and mom to argue from time to time. And she was told that Mikey would get what he deserved.

All Claire knew for sure was that she was all alone. She was scared and confused and now she was supposed to call these people that she didn't even know "mom and dad." And suddenly she had a sister. Who are these people?

But that was then. And the now was beckoning come. Come if you dare. Open the box a wee bit further, but know this, you can never fully shut it again! So with a deep sigh Claire flung open the box.

She wanted names of the investigators closest to the case. To ask them questions of course, but first, so she could profile them. That would tell her a lot about whether the contents of their respective files could be trusted or not. She'd been around too long to not know that coverups and shoddy work were often the rule rather than the exception. Slam dunk. Next!

Slowly she began to profile anyone involved in her brother's case. Much of what she found was expected. But not everything. It seems that one detective wasn't exactly on board with the others even though he eventually acquiesced. And that's who she needed to talk to. She'd heard rumblings that her brother may not have been the "evil" person that he had been made out to be. In fact, his life in prison was exemplary, rather contradictory if he was indeed a monster.

O'MALLEY

So Claire began to reach out and soon found that detective O'Malley, now retired, still lived in Portland and could be found daily out along the seaboard. He and his Tom Cat 6.2. She had done a little sailing herself so that might just be an "in" if she needed one. She decided that she'd show up in person rather than call ahead. Eyeball to eyeball. Then she'd know!

Claire got up the next morning still unsure if she could go through with it. The thought of seeing her brother for the first time in, oh my God, thirty years! How was that possible? She was eleven at the time, he was fifteen. They were babies, and now she was planning on meeting her forty five year old brother!

But first, O'Malley. So she dressed for the occasion. If she read him correctly he might well pull something on her and invite her out for a cruise just to test her a little. By God, if he did, she'd be ready! She'd learned a thing or two about dealing with these curmudgeons. Maybe he wasn't one but she'd be ready just in case. Right down to the deck shoes. Bring it on, O'Malley!

As if he didn't know who she was! He knew someone would show up eventually, but it should have been thirty years ago, for

God's sake! He'd tried to bring attention to the case back then but he was shut down by his captain and told to never speak of it again. Or else. Well, he needed his job and he'd toe the line, but if anyone starting sniffing around and he got wind of it, he'd be the first one in line to take a stroll down memory lane!

He'd gotten to know Mikey, and often went up to visit him at the prison. Yeah, he'd committed the crime, no doubt about it, but the most he should have got was manslaughter. Everyone knew what a bastard their dad was, and he got what he deserved. Everyone knew it! But, the pressure was on to close the case quickly. The force didn't need the attention and the sooner it was swept under the rug, the better. Besides, he did the crime so he needed to do the time! Fine. But life without parole? Come on. What a bunch of gutless bureaucrats. O'Malley nearly quit after that debacle, but crap, he needed the job. What else was there to say?

So he stayed on, rose through the ranks, and eventually retired early. One can only stand so much odour, and he knew if he hadn't left when he did, he'd either succumb to it entirely or he'd open a hornet's nest they'd never be able to contain. God, he wanted to. But it gets lonely when you're all alone. Except when he was out sailing. That was different. And it was time to go right now.

He spotted her before she saw him. Striking indeed, and he had to chuckle, she had dressed as if she were going sailing! He liked her already but he'd make her work for it a bit! Maybe she had profiled him but he'd had his eye on her for years! There were a few such cases of justice denied, and he was hellbent on being part of the eventually solution of every one of them, even if it meant he had to drop a clue or two here and there. And that's exactly what happened here! It helps to have contacts, and he had no lack of them.

"Hey, are you O'Malley?"

"Who's asking?" Like he didn't know.

"My names Claire. I'm an Investigative Journalist with the Post. I'd like to ask you a few questions."

"And why would I talk to you?"

"Why wouldn't you? I heard that you're a pretty straight shooter. And besides, you're retired now so there's nothing they can do to you."

"Who's "they," friend?" O'Malley like her style.

Claire was moving way too fast. Damn, I know better than that! I need this guy on my side.

"I'm sorry, I shouldn't have said that. I'm looking into a case that you worked on thirty years ago and I was hoping you could help me out."

"And why would I do that?"

"Because the case stinks, and it stunk even worse back then. And I've been told that you were one of the best in the business back then. I was told that this case was a thorn in your side, and still is, according to my source. I'm talking about the Michael Godfrey case. You know which one, I'm sure."

And he did indeed. And crap, he liked this woman. Aggressive or what! Definitely his style but he wasn't going to let her off that easy.

"You a sailor?"

"I've done some sailing. Is that your rig?"

Like she didn't already know that.

"Yep. I'm about to go for a cruise. There's enough room for the both of us. Let's go."

"OK, but I need your help."

"Come on. We'll talk later."

And that's what they did. He put the Tom Cat through its paces. She hung in there like the trouper he knew she was. This was going to be fun! And oh yes, they'd be talking real soon!

It became obvious that they had both checked the other out thoroughly before this meeting ever took place. And it was equally obvious that they respected each other. There would be no more games between these two!

O'Malley was adamant that Claire know all the facts, not just the file version, before she went to see her brother. Her father was well known to the police and in fact, had a sheet a mile long. But that fact was not admitted into evidence. That was just for starters.

Michael Godfrey. 15 years old. Murdered father with two shots from a double barrel shotgun. Called 911 and waited for police to arrive. Taken into custody without incident. Pleaded guilty to first degree murder. Avoided the death penalty but received life without parole.

There was a bit more, but essentially, that was it. All wrapped up. A slam dunk.

Except that wasn't quite the way it went down. Now it was thirty years later and all hell was about to break loose! Why? Because everyone who was part of that crappy deal was still alive and O'Malley could barely contain himself! Oh happy day!

But of course it wasn't a happy day. This young man had spent the last thirty years locked up like an animal. He needed to pay for his crime. No one would deny that, but had the same investigators who built a case against Mikey been on his defence team, he may well have walked. Neither scenario was acceptable but that mattered not to the powers that be, and Mikey was thrown away.

Until now. And with Claire on the scene, well, O'Malley could hardly contain himself! He knew the files he had secretly filed away in a "safe" place would one day bear fruit, and it was nearly harvest time!

That's where they began. One file after another slowly shook off its' cobwebs and came alive under the relentless stare of those who had disturbed their sleep. They spewed forth their secrets so they might finally rest in peace, finally free from their deep, dark secrets. Claire had been privy over the years to many such files but this was different. This was her life revealed; her families portrait brought to life in front of her very eyes. And she didn't like what she was seeing.

No wonder her mom had not been there for her. And her father? My God! He was vile; he had a record a mile long: child molester, thief, drug dealer, and on and on and on. Yet, somehow, she had thought of him as her hero! Her daddy, who could do anything! Claire involuntarily shivered, and she could not contain the tears that made their way down to the tip of her chin. O'Malley silently watched her, as she devolved into the small child of yesterday, and then he watched as she re-evolved to the powerful person she was today. At that moment he knew he was on the right side of this issue. This woman would not be stopped! And he was going for the ride!

"I want to see my brother." That's what he liked about her. Straight to the point. He had spent hours with Claire by this time, telling her about his many meetings with Mikey over the years. How they had become close friends despite him being on the other side. She learned of Mikey's guardian angel that had appeared the day he was incarcerated, in the form of a huge black guy by the name of Charlie. Charlie was a lifer but had given his life to Jesus some 40 years prior. And he'd walked straight ever since. It didn't change a thing as far as the authorities were concerned, but it probably saved the lives of hundreds of inmates over the years. In fact, he had eventually became an ordained minister.

CHARLEY

When Mikey arrived he was destined to become a boy toy to more than just a few of the sex starved inmates. But that didn't happen. Charley made sure of that. He had heard about the new arrival and was determined to get to him before any of the crazies did. And even though he was a pastor, he was as big as a tank, and more than a few of the inmates had experienced the wrath of Charlie when he "temporarily" set aside his collar. He was feared and yet loved at the same time. Even if you had crossed Charley and he'd had a little backroom chat with you, the next day he'd be there for you if you needed him. Respected? Big time!

Mikey didn't know it at the time but Charley had just saved his life! And he was about to learn a whole lot more than he ever wanted to about the prison system.

Charley had seen it all inside these walls. Hell, he'd been one of the bad guys, the real bad guys. Not only had he seen it all; he'd done it all, and he'd regretted it ever since. He'd moved on but a lot of these guys hadn't, and as far as they were concerned, anything goes. They weren't getting out anyway. So what if they tacked on a couple more life sentences. Big deal!

So Mikey had better watch out or he was theirs, plain and simple. Charley may have been big, and he may have been mean, but he was only one guy . . .

And that's how it went for Mikey. He was a prisoner within a prison. Never, ever go anywhere alone, especially the can, or the showers, or the laundry room, or the . . . and so on.

And that was tough. Most of the guards were quite happy to see a little action from time to time, and this kid, well one day he'd get his! So if Charley thought he had his work cut out for him before, now he'd become a full time babysitter!

And a teacher! And like it or not, Mikey was going to know Jesus, whether he wanted to or not! That turned out to be the easy part. Apparently his grandma was a real Bible thumper from way back and Mikey was taught a whole lot of Bible verses that he could call on whenever he got into a "situation." Her words.

So when Mikey pulled the trigger that night, he'd already done some praying, but prayer or not, he was determined that his family was going to be free from that monster. And if anyone thought he felt bad about what he'd done, well, they were wrong!

He was smart enough to know that he had forfeited his earthly life, but he was pretty convinced that God still loved him despite what he had done. He knew that didn't make it right and that there are always consequences for one's actions, but he figured he'd probably have the rest of his life to make those amends. Never once had it occurred to him that they might execute him. That is, until his court appointed lawyer brought it up. That scared the pants off him and made it rather easy for him to just plead guilty with the promise that it would all go away. As long as he co-operated.

Charley wasn't about to let Mikey off easy though. Before the first day had passed Charley had assigned him some reading assignments straight out of the Bible. "That's just to get you started. And, young man, you're going to finish high school as well."

"What's the point? I'm not getting out of here anyway. Why bother!"

"That's a load of crap! You don't know that! And besides, what else you got to do that's so important? Answer me that!"

And that's when Mikey began to get it. Besides, if he got on Charley's bad side, he could end up out there, with them. He was a quick learner, this boy!

He'd just graduated from junior high and was about to enter senior high in the fall, except that wasn't going to happen now. At least not at the school he should have been attending. Instead, and he would thank Charley for it later, he was given permission to take the rest of his high school by correspondent courses; that or nothing. With Charley breathing down his neck that was a no brainer.

But with no distractions such as girls and friends to hang around with, Mikey excelled in his studies, and in fact, finished up the final three years in less than two. And, his marks put him on the honour roll, although that was kept rather quiet, him being in prison and all.

Charley had a three point plan for Mikey and he was going to follow it. No ifs, ands, or buts! And it wasn't up for discussion! Plus these would all happen simultaneously.

In Charley's words " you're gonna get your high school diploma, you're gonna learn the Bible inside out, and you're gonna work out every day until you can stand up for yourself! And that's final!" And that's the way it went. Charley was the boss. He knew it and so did Mikey!

Mikey had pretty much levelled out at about the 6 foot mark when he arrived but he needed some filling out, at least that was Charley's take. "If you're gonna survive in here, you need some meat on those bones, and I don't mean fat either!" And with that in mind, they headed to the gym. One thing about prisons, they always have a gym! This place is your friend. It doesn't talk back and it'll take anything you can give it. Use it and abuse it if you have to, but you'd better be here every flipping day! You slack off and the wolf pack out there will eat you up. "Got it?"

He got it alright. It took awhile, but over the next few years Mikey's physique went from that of a snot nosed beanpole to that of an Arnold Schwartzennegar wannabe. As tough as Charley was , he was one proud papa. "Yep! That's my boy! Now get back to work!"

Charley contacted the Ministerial Association that he belonged to to arrange for Mikey to begin training as a pastor. He and Mikey had talked at length about God. After seeing the impact Charley had on so many of the inmates lives, it was an easy decision for Mikey to make. He knew God would be there with him the whole time. He just didn't know it would manifest itself this way. And Charley couldn't have been prouder!

Seminary studies came easily to Mikey. Where Charley had struggled as if against giants, this young man owned them. And what an attitude he had! And this was in prison! Just imagine what Mikey could accomplish given half a chance in the outside world. And that made Charley sad. So much potential . . .

"Oops! Guess I'd better listen to my own advice. We're here, and there's a hell of a need right here, and God loves these guys just as much as anyone else, so get to it, buttercups. Yeah, me, and you too, Charlie Brown!" He snickered at his own lame joke. "And besides, Charlie Brown don't even spell his own name right!" And he snickered again, making sure no one was around to hear him. After all, he had a reputation to uphold, and snickering? Well, that just wouldn't cut it!

By the time Mikey graduated from Seminary, he had been at the prison for about eight years, and in that time, he had earned darn near as much respect as Charley commanded. He was a gentle soul, and despite the way he had been treated earlier on, he bore no grudge towards others and began to mirror Charley's work, albeit in his own unique way. Kind of like a one two punch. If Charley's way wasn't working well with some individual, or vice versa, the other would take him on, and give it a shot. These two had went from a mentor/protege relationship to a relationship of equals. There was no doubt that each loved and respected the other.

Around Mikey's tenth year of incarceration it became evident that a changing of the guard was taking place. And finally, Charley forced a sit down with Mikey. "We need to talk."

Mikey had weaved and bobbed as long as he could but he knew the "talk" was inevitable. "I'm really busy. Can we do it next week? I have a lot on my plate over the next few days."

"No, we can't. Go do what you gotta do but tonight it's us. Mano Mano. Got it?" And of course he did. He respected Charley far too much. But this was a conversation he didn't want to have.

CLAIRE AND MIKEY MEET

O'Malley made the call and lined up the meeting on Claire's behalf. It was the least he could do. He'd gotten to know her pretty well these last few days and man, she was as tough as they come, but this was different. And personal. And she was scared. He knew it and she knew it. Neither had to say anything, but both knew they were in this thing together. Like it or not, she had begun to lean on him as though he were her father, well not her father, but like a father should be. He liked it and she needed him. Good.

Mikey knew he was getting a visitor. O'Malley had contacted him but was vague on the details. Curious. But if there was one person he respected nearly as much as Charley, it was O'Malley. He never could figure out why he had taken such an interest in him. But he kept showing up to visit him. No one else ever did, that is, until the last couple of years when some of the inmates were released and had sung his praises to their families. After that, every now and then he'd have a visitor, sometimes a family member just wanting to thank him for taking care of their boy, and on occasion, the former inmate himself just wanting to say thanks. But, he sensed that this was different. It made him nervous and that was not like him. Not one bit!

The closer they got to the prison the more nervous Claire became. Maybe this was a mistake. I should have come years ago. I abandoned my own brother. He's going to hate me. I'm such a coward. I hate me! And on and on it went. O'Malley wanted to wrap her in his arms and hold her close, let her scream, or whatever. He hated seeing her this way. If she needed a father figure in her life, he wanted the job, and one way or another, he was staying close to this girl!

Oh God! There it is! I thought it was further away. Calm down girl. Breathe. And finally she became Claire, the Investigator, once again. She had a job to do. She'd done this dozens of times in the past. No big deal! Except, it was. It was a really big deal, and suddenly once again, she was a really little girl. Thank God O'Malley was with her because the chances are she would have got back in the vehicle and got the hell out of there!

"We're here to see Michael Godfrey. We have an appointment."

Cell phones, recording devices, wallets, etc., pat down, the usual and finally they were escorted to the visitors area. O'Malley moved off to the tiny sitting area hugging the far wall while Claire sat at the table waiting for her brother's arrival.

She could hear him coming before she saw him. She composed herself as best as she could and waited for . . . she wasn't sure what she was waiting for. Any semblance of a suntan that she had when she arrived at the prison had long since gone on vacation. She glanced at the door as it slowly began to open, quickly fluffing up her hair for the fortieth time in the last thirty seconds, and squaring her body up for the assault she was sure was coming. And then he walked in.

He stopped. They stared at each other. And each began to cry. Unabashedly. Not a word was spoken for what seemed an eternity. And then he stepped forward and sat down across from Claire, his baby sister! "Thank you, God!" Over and over he repeated it, "Thank you, God! Thank you, God!" They weren't allowed to embrace but they could hold each other's hands and when they finally touched, what little control Claire had mustered up to that point evaporated completely.

Control be damned. They had found each other. That's all that mattered. Big brother; baby sister. United at last.

O'Malley could barely contain himself. He was pretty sure it would go well but this blew the socks of any scenario he had imagined. And they hadn't even spoken yet! Thank you God for letting me be part of this!

Suddenly Claire blurted out "I love you!" and quickly covered her mouth with her hand. What did I just do?

Mikey began to chuckle and then he roared. And he cried. But these were tears of joy! Pure, unadulterated joy! "I love you too!" And he burst out laughing again, but this time she was right there with him. Two kids having the time of their lives! And then they both looked over at O'Malley and they began to roar.

Thirty years gone in the blink of an eye! But at this moment they were 11 and 15 and all was well with the world! But it wasn't, and in very short order their lives would change forever.

They were there an hour but it felt as if a minute. She didn't want to leave; he didn't want her to go, but they were in different worlds. And that was reality. With tears unabashedly running down both their cheeks, they went their separate ways, she promising to return real soon. "I love you!"

And as the door closed behind him, she heard him call out "I love you, sis!"

She was a wreck. Thank God O'Malley was driving. Thank God for O'Malley period. He was her rock, a job he was quite happy to take on. Claire would stick around one more day but then she had to get back to Seattle. And besides, she missed Derek like crazy!

So now Claire had another mission on top of all the other missions she already had on the go. But this was personal. That was her brother in there, and if there was any way on God's green earth that she could get him out of there, she'd find it. Don't ever underestimate the power of a woman!

MIKEY AFTER CLAIRE'S VISIT

When Mikey went back to his quarters (cell) he was barely able to function. A few of the inmates asked him who his visitor was but he barely remembered responding to their queries. That confused them as well because the Mikey they knew always had plenty to say. Now there was nothing. And when he went into his cell and closed the door behind him, which he never did, they knew something was up. And that's how gossip gets started.

Maybe he was being transferred. Some had heard that he was being granted bail. There was even a rumour floating around that his sister was here to visit him. None could remember him ever even mentioning family. And now he wasn't talking.

If they were confused it paled in comparison to what Mikey was going through at that moment. After all these years. Not one inquiry from the outside world. In fact, his only contact on the outside, aside from his ministry work, was O'Malley. That's who he needed to talk to. Why hadn't he told him so he could have been more prepared. Prepared for what he wasn't sure. And what would he have done differently?

"My God, I have a sister!" He'd been told a couple of years after he arrived in this place that both his Mom and his sister had passed away. End of story. He had no reason not to believe it, besides, it made it easier being in this joint when he had no life outside it anyway. He continued " And she came looking for me! And she told me she loved me!" and he began to sob silently, and then he began to bawl, burying his face in his pillow lest anyone hear him.

Dinner time came and went, and still Mikey did not emerge. The other inmates were becoming concerned. "Maybe he's sick. Someone's got to check on him. Jerry, you're the closest thing he has to a buddy in here. Go check." And Jerry did.

"Hey Mikey, its Jerry. Can I come in?"

No answer. Mikey lay with his back to the door.

"Mikey, I'm coming in." and he made his way over to his friend. "Are you ok, buddy? Everyone's worried about you."

A muffled reply "I'm fine. I just need to think. I'll see you all tomorrow. I need to sleep. Close the door when you leave, ok?" And with that, Mikey pulled the blankets up and over his head.

This was not the Mikey he knew. He'd never heard him sound like that. "I think he's crying." to himself. "Jeez, now I'm getting scared."

These may have been lifers but they were still human, and they cared for each other in each their own way. Oh, they had their disagreements alright, and things became downright violent from time to time, but there was still a brotherhood at work here. And right now they were concerned for one of their own.

Jerry took it a little further and asked one of the guards if he knew what had happened. "Yeah, his sister came to visit him today. That's all I know."

His sister. Mikey never talked much about life outside these walls but he distinctly remembered him telling some of the guys that his family was all dead. He had no one. "You guys are my family." And that was that.

Now what? He hadn't even considered ever being outside these walls. He liked it here. He knew everyone, not that he liked everyone, but he knew them all. He knew what to expect from them, and they knew his boundaries as well. One big, happy family. Maybe not happy, but definitely family.

I wonder what Charley would do? "Charley I need you." he whispered to himself. "What am I supposed to do?" But really, what was there to do? He was a lifer with no chance of parole. Claire had alluded to the fact that he had been screwed over. There was a case to be made. Don't give up. We're in this together. He didn't know how to reply. He was barely able to acknowledge her but there she was, as real as he. And he'd told her that he loved her! The words had just come out. And he'd cried in front of her! And once again, he began to sob.

The next day, any evidence of his odd behaviour was gone and Mikey was back to being the Mikey they knew. To their great relief! They needed this guy! Anybody messing with him was messing with us, and that ain't gonna end well for anyone!

Mikey never spoke of it again to the inmates, including Jerry. But, he was quick to contact O'Malley. "I need to see you. You owe me an explanation."

O'Malley had been expecting the call, and a couple of days after Claire had left, he made his way back to the prison. They needed to talk. A talk he'd wanted to have a long time ago, but now that he knew Claire would be there for Mikey, the time was right.

All Claire could do on the trip home was repeat over and over "I have a brother! I have a brother!" over and over again. And she'd told him she loved him. And he said the same thing to her. " I need to do something. I'm coming for you Mikey!" And she giggled to herself. "Where do I begin?"

JASON REMINISCES AS THE 4TH ANN. APPROACHES

How time flies! Their fourth year anniversary was fast approaching. Unbelievable! Oh, Janice had her doubts a time or two, but her friends were in absolute awe of Jason. Mr. Perfect! But she knew him better than they, and though he was all those things they fawned over, it was just too perfect. Yet, other than that one really weird episode, he was a great husband. "That's the problem with being a writer." she mused under her breath, "we're always looking for the story behind the facade." So once again, she shook it off and made plans for the big night.

Of course, Jason was the benefactor of all Janice's busyness. He knew she had been "observing" him more than usual these past few months, but lately that had dropped off significantly. Of course, he had worked the "perfect husband" routine to the max. He may not have known much about women on a personal level, but he was learning quickly. Of course, being a psychologist with a rather busy practice certainly didn't hurt. Oh how people loved to tell him their stories! Women especially!

Perhaps if he just quit right now. After all, he hadn't "acted out" since after their honeymoon, nearly four years, although he had "observed" women on many occasions in the intervening years. Still, he hadn't "acted out" so maybe he was finally done with that dark chapter. Maybe they could have a good life, after all. He said the words, but even as he said them, he knew that that would not be his reality. He'd suppressed the urges time and time and again, but in his heart of hearts he knew the inevitable was approaching, and there wasn't a damn thing he could do about it! Besides, he still had one cross left.

Jason was no fool. He held a Doctorate in Psychology and ensured he was always up on the latest advancements in his field. He counted among his friends medical doctors, psychiatrists, and the like. These were the kinds of subjects they spent hours debating amongst themselves. But still he found himself observing them closely. Perhaps they too, had secret lives. Secrets that they dare not share lest they be exposed. He wondered if they too, observed him as he observed them. One would be a fool to think otherwise. And with that constantly in mind, Jason was always extremely careful of what he said. If anyone could detect something even slightly out of place, it would be this group.

How he wished he could ask them! Of course that was impossible, for to do so would immediately raise suspicion and that's the last thing he wanted. Better to talk about them; after all, they, (him included), were a bunch of narcissists anyway, and what better subject than themselves.

But he had a greater concern. He wished he didn't, but he did. God. And that bothered him to no end. Despite him being a psychopath, if that's indeed what he was, he knew God was real. That didn't fit the psychology very well but he knew that one day he would be held accountable for his actions. He'd resigned himself to the fact that there would be consequences if/when he were caught. Probably jail, possibly execution. Those he could live with, and he laughed at the absurdity of what he had just uttered.

But eternal damnation, complete separation from God, that was quite another matter. And yet here he was contemplating another kill and at the same time, trying to figure out how God would ultimately judge him. "Yep, I'm definitely a psycho!"

Every time he looked at a cross, regardless of where it was, he felt "saved." And yet the crosses he possessed were instruments of death. Death at his hands. The cross should have been a symbol of God's enduring sacrifice. A symbol of God's endless love. He tried to remember how this had all begun. His Mom had treated her cross with great reverence; in fact he had never seen her remove it. He loved fiddling with it whenever she held him in her lap and read the Bible to him or sung Bible songs. He especially liked "Jesus loves me, this I know, for the Bible tells me so . . . He could never get very far with this tune, even today, before the tears would begin to flow. "Mommy, I miss you so much."

He remembered when he was first given the cross that his Mom had worn. It alone had survived the fire that had torn through their home that fateful night so long ago. They had retrieved it from the ashes and it was eventually given to him as a reminder of his Mom. In fact, it soon overtook him. Even thought it was obviously a cross worn by a woman, he adopted it and wore it under his clothing. In some perverse way, his Mom would always be with him. Like her family would always be with her because of the crosses she had brought with her from Guatemala. That's when he knew what to do with the crosses.

At the time it seemed a rather dumb thing to do, but as time went by, the crosses seemed to speak to him. The first time he'd placed a cross on his victim it seemed the right thing to do. She was so pretty, just like his mommy. Just like his mommy was before she became a bad mommy. He could feel himself becoming angrier and angrier as his thoughts took him to that very dark place. "She deserved it!"

After that, it just made sense. And after the next kill, it became a must. "What if I run out of crosses? I'll have to find some more crosses! But they have to be the same as Mommy's!" And he did try but to no avail. But this was crazy talk. He wasn't going to kill anymore. He was done. "I need to throw the other ones away. And try he did, but he couldn't do it! They owned him and he knew it. "Ok, but when they're gone, that's it!" to himself. And so the safety deposit box housed the remaining crosses until they would once again be called upon to relinquish their treasure.

But Jason had will power, no question. He wrestled his demons, and although tempted on many occasions, he resisted for four long years. And that's about the time when he met Janice and she led him into a life he never believed he could have. Suddenly he wanted no more to do with the darkness of his yesterdays. But he still kept the two remaining crosses. He didn't know why, but what harm? They were locked away in a safety deposit box. Out of sight, out of mind. Made sense. Except to a psychopath!

And that's where they stayed. Until after their honeymoon, that is. But once again, he found himself in front of the safety deposit box for the first time in four years. Resignedly, he opened the box. There was nothing else in the box except the two remaining crosses and a few documents. When he relocked the box but one remained. He had tried so hard. But it wasn't enough.

Had they not been in his possession he may have been able to resist the temptation longer, but that was doubtful. The tiny cross he had worn since a small child teased him constantly. On numerous occasions he had nearly ripped it from his neck to save himself from being strangled. He knew that was impossible but the self imposed marks on his neck suggested otherwise. And seeing "her" on the beach some two weeks prior had triggered something far bigger than himself. Now he had the extra cross tucked neatly away in his jacket pocket and he knew he would be giving it away very soon! That turned out to be January 11th, 2011. Then there was one cross left.

JOLINE HOME FOR THE ANNIVERSARY

Joline had been home on a couple more occasions after the "freak out" session when her mom had tried to sidestep her questions. She had to admit that perhaps her Mom really was just uptight over the book tour. It was certainly understandable, and perhaps her gut feeling was just that, a feeling. In any case, her Mom seemed perfectly happy, and couldn't wait to have the family all together to help them celebrate their fourth anniversary!

So she pushed her intuition to the side, after all, this was about her Mom and Jason, not her. Perhaps her time would come one day, but secretly, she hoped it was a long way off! It's not like she didn't date; it just wasn't a priority. She could have brought a date with her for this occasion but she knew that would lead to all sorts of questions, especially by her Grammy and Grampy, and that would be totally unfair to her date. Sorry guys, I am not ready to settle down anytime soon!

It's not like she didn't get the attention. She was one of those rare people that not only had the looks, but had the personality that attracted everyone around her. It was obvious that she spent a lot of time outdoors. Her blonde hair swept her tanned face and those eyes, emerald in colour would best describe them, and the smile. The smile that would break many hearts before she was done! Not that she would do that on purpose, but it was bound to happen.

Joline never seemed to understand the charisma that she possessed. Perhaps it was her humble nature. Humble indeed, but driven, and a fierce opponent if one wronged her or something she stood for, and an incredible advocate for anything concerned with social justice and the environment.

She had indeed become her own person. A person others could depend on, a role she gladly embraced. Even though she was but twenty two, she had the wisdom of someone much older. She credited her Mom for allowing her to fly at such a young age. Go out into the world. Make mistakes, but please, learn from them. Don't let anyone, including me, set limits on you!

Her grandparents had done the same for her Mom. They had helped her to find her wings when she was broken. They didn't push her but they gently nudged her towards the door. She remembered her Mom telling her "Your Grampy and Grammy loved me where I was. They didn't condemn me but they made sure they didn't enable me either. I'd have to learn to fly on my own but they'd be close by to assist me when I stumbled." She continued "And I did stumble a few times, but they picked me up, brushed me off, and gently kicked my butt out the door. You've got this honey, I believe in you, and so do they. We are all so proud of you!"

Joline hugged her Mom. Her Mom was her rock. And if anything ever happened to her rock . . .

The Anniversary dinner went off without a hitch. The couple seemed so in love. Her grandparents loved Jason, and he seemed to reciprocate. And he doted on her Mom. How could she have been so wrong! She wanted to apologize to him for her suspicions but that would have been dumb. No foul, no harm. Leave it alone.

The weekend ended all too quickly and Joline was off. Final semester! And then there were choices to make. She was one of the fortunate few, fortunate because she had earned that right, and had several incredible opportunities from which to choose. The world was her oyster and she could hardly wait to partake of its treasures.

JANICE AFTER THE ANNIVERSARY

That had gone well. As far as everyone was concerned they were the perfect couple. Even Joline had to concede that they were meant for each other. As much as Janice tried to convince herself, she didn't buy it. They were anything but perfect. In fact, they were too perfect. Almost robotic. Jason always said the right things. He always bought the right wine. He always bought the right gifts. His hair was perfect. So was his suit. It drove her nuts!

In her crazy moments, she could imagine that his daytimer was filled with post it notes saying things like "do this now" or "If she says this, you say that" or any one of a hundred commands that any good robot could understand. Thank God she wasn't a drinker! Just imagine what she would come up with if she were drunk!" She had to chuckle at the absurdity of it all.

JASON AFTER THE ANNIVERSARY

He knew they were all fooled. All but Janice, that is. Yet, they never talked about it. They made their way around the elephant in the room quite nicely, thank you very much. Jason knew that Janice wasn't as smart as he, I mean, who was? But she had that sense, that gut feeling that was beginning to concern him. He'd never tripped up, other than that one time, but he knew that she was onto him. Why'd he ever marry her? How stupid of me!

Her behaviour was really beginning to annoy him. "If I lose it again, and I'm pretty damn close, it'll all be your fault! Don't you forget that!" to himself.

"I'm going for a walk. Need anything from the store?" And off he went before she could even answer.

She knew he was peed. Too bad. Jerk! And all that without even a word being spoken.

A marriage made in Paradise. Paradise lost, that is. Hell she was as big a hypocrite as he. They pretended well, these two. We should be so proud of ourselves! And the elephant nodded.

It wasn't like she needed him financially, or he her for that matter. And they certainly weren't emotionally supporting the other. And yet neither would make the move. Instead, they celebrated their 4th year facade. Oh happy us! Toast, anyone?

Few had ever seen Jason angry. Even he didn't like himself when he got that way. Control freaks are supposed to be in control, but had anyone seen him at this moment, they may well have run the other way. Thank God it was night for he was not a pretty sight. "I'll kill you! Don't think I won't." under his breath.

It took another hour for Jason to settle down. Oh my God, I'm losing it! "Please God, help me. Please help me."

When he returned home, Janice had already gone to bed. "Thank goodness" he muttered to himself. He'd retire to the study for a while, perhaps have a glass of wine or two before he too retired for the evening. They were going to have to do something. This situation was untenable. He knew it and she knew it.

Jason tried to analyze the last few hours. He'd never lost it quite like that before and it scared him. My God, he'd even threatened to kill Janice, even if it was just said to himself. He would never do that! He loved her! Didn't he? He knew he loved himself. That was a given. I love her. I do.

When Jason finally made his way to bed, Janice was already fast asleep. He studied her, as he would any of his subjects. Just what exactly does she think she knows? What could she know? There was nothing to know. Jason sat down in the rocker next to the bed and for the next several hours he stared at his sleeping wife. "I love you, I love you not . . . I love you, I love you not . . . " over and over. Finally he undressed and fell in to bed exhausted.

LA PUSH

"Good morning Sweetheart! There she stood, breakfast tray in hand. You were snoring and I didn't want to wake you, so I decided to serve you breakfast in bed this morning! Here, have some coffee!"

His first thoughts were "I don't snore." But instead, "Thanks hon, what a surprise!" And it was. Maybe she'd poisoned the orange juice! Okay, that's not fair. If anything, it would be him doing the poisoning!

He studied her as he ate. She looked so happy. Was he just losing it? Or was she just playing some elaborate game to throw him off? He needed to go to work. Now.

"Jason, I was thinking . . . "

"Oh great" under his breath. "About?"

"I was thinking that we should take a few days off. We've both been working so hard and we barely see each other except when we're ready to fall into bed. It's affecting us. I know it's affecting me. It's got to be affecting you too! We need to have some fun!" What happened to the other Janice?

He wanted to shut her down right then and there but that would have been dumb. "You know babe, I've been thinking the same thing."

"You have? I knew it! Let's go away this weekend. Please."

How does one say no to that? One doesn't. And so they made plans for the weekend. Just the two of them; the elephant stays home!

In retrospect, she'd question herself about this decision until her dying day, but this was now, and she desperately wanted her marriage to work. She was used to doing everything to the max, and she'd certainly do the same to save their marriage. She was all in. Hopefully Jason felt the same way! If this didn't work. . . . She knew he'd never go to counselling. After all, he was a counsellor; forget that! What could they tell him that he didn't already know? He was weird like that.

So this was their best shot. They'd always love exploring along the beaches at La Push so decided they'd push it a little further this time and tackle the South Coast Wilderness Trail which ran from La Push (Third Beach) to the Hoh River, about 17.5 miles based on their travel guide. They'd stay the first night at Forks, which they'd done a couple of times before. Forks had become a really big deal with the Twilight phenomena, but now that that had finally died down, the place was sane once again. Quaint, really. A step back in time.

They had hiked various portions up and down the coast but usually the shorter portions which just took a few hours. This was was more intense but they were both up for the task. When Jason had mentioned this particular trail, Janice was all in. It would require them spending one night camping on the beach, but that would be no big deal, and besides, the scenery would be spectacular. A final push the next morning would take them to the end of this portion of the trail which ended at the Hoh River.

Suddenly these two were talking again and going through their checklists, tent, cooking utensils, matches, first aid kit, and so on. Oh yes, make sure you pack a bottle of wine. Gotta have that for the camping night. And they both began to giggle. When was the last time they did that?

Janice snuggled into the crook of Jason's arms and they held each other tightly. This was the way it was supposed to be! A glass of wine capped off a perfect evening. Now, if they could just learn to hit play; rewind; play again; they'd be fine. Maybe, just maybe everything would be fine.

Their home was a joy the next morning. The elephant was nowhere to be found and with just two more sleeps to go, there was plenty of work still to be done. So off Jason went and Janice headed for her study. She may work at home but she was as disciplined as anyone that punched a clock. Besides, they both had 2 days to accomplish 5 days of work!

The next two days whizzed by and finally they pulled out of the driveway. They must have checked their list fifty times, this rather anal couple, but now it was time. Two kids in a convertible barreling down the highway . . .

Two and a half hours to Port Angeles. Stop for lunch, another hour or so to Forks depending on how many times they stopped. The scenery was seductive; it was impossible not to stop for photos. Moss climbed into tree tops, and the glass like lakes took ones breath away. The slight chill in the air completed the mood.

And final, Forks, the home of Edward and Bella, and Jacob, of Twilight fame. Thankfully, summer was over and the groupies of all ages were long since gone home.

So they booked into their room, strolled throughout the town, and went for dinner at Forks favourite haunt. It would be early to bed for this couple as tomorrow's hike would be no cake walk. And because they needed a really good sleep, that pretty well guaranteed that they wouldn't get one. And they didn't. But no matter. Nothing was going to hold these two back.

And what a start! They'd decided to leave their car at the hotel and take a cab out to La Push rather than leave it overnight. Too isolated, convertible top, not worth the risk. They both loved the sound of the crashing waves as they made their way down to ground zero. Huge, nearly white driftwood threatened to block their path as they nimbly made their way to the beckoning ocean mere yards away. And how they loved the seastacks, particularly the so called Giants Graveyard. How many thousands of photos must have been taken of these behemoths! And there was Teawhit Head and further to the east stood Taylor Point. Many a ship had strayed to close to shore in these waters and run aground, hundreds, if memory serves me right.

And finally they were able to dip their toes in the ocean. Officially, their hike had begun! The scenery is stunning in this area and they had to constantly remind themselves that they were alone out here. This would not be a great place to have a mishap, and slips or falls were a constant threat. Pay attention, hike for a time and then stop and admire the view. It wasn't overly difficult for an experienced hiker but caution was still the keyword.

Also, though time overall was not a huge factor, there was one window that best not be ignored. The tide chart would see to that but their job was to arrive as per tide schedule less they get smashed against the rocks or find themselves out at sea. Get through this area safely and the rest, while not easy, could be at whatever pace they choose.

That would be no issue for these two. So naturally, they arrived at low tide and made their way around the imposing boulders with no issue. Once on the other side they'd decide where they wanted to set up camp for the night. The day was young but there was no hurry. They were all alone. Why not set up camp, do a little beachcombing and enjoy that bottle of wine they had packed. The sunset to come would be mesmerizing, and the wine should ensure a most enjoyable evening.

Two people in love. What could be better! This is exactly what the Doctor had ordered!

Even Jason had to concede that as much as he had reluctantly went along with Janice's suggestion, as it drew closer, he had gotten more and more excited. And now, he couldn't imagine being in a better place or with anybody but Janice. He drew her closer to him, wrapped the thermal blanket snugly over their shoulders, and told her how much he loved her. And he meant it! It even surprised him. But he did mean it. Every word.

She snuggled even closer and they stayed like that until the sun dropped over the horizon. If there was ever a God moment, it was now. But finally, with a chill in the air, they made their way into the tent they would call home this night. What a wonderful night!

The early morning light beckoned them awake. Come and discover the treasures that await you. Tide pools exposed by the receding waters revealed their secrets for this couple to see.

A couple of bald eagles lounged nearby, sea gulls filled the air, sea cucumbers, starfish, and a thousand other creatures that claimed the tide pools as their home shared their humble abode with Janice and Jason. Grab this moment in time for soon it will be gone.

Although neither felt like eating, they thought it wise as there were still a few hours to go. Then they packed up, garbage included, and made their way towards the Hoh River. The second leg of the journey proved as wonderful as the first, and though somewhat fatigued, neither wanted this journey to end. What a glorious weekend! From here they'd catch a shuttle back to La Push, stay one more night and head back to Seattle in the morning.

And that's how that went. Janice was beside herself! Jason was confused. By this time he had self diagnosed and was convinced he was a psychopath, and yet, he could barely wipe the smile off his face. He was in love. He knew it and he also felt it! Now what?

JASON'S FINAL KILL

But then it was back to the grind. As far as Janice was concerned, the mini holiday was just what the doctor ordered!

"I knew it was just my imagination!" Janice was beside herself! "I knew he still loved me! And I love him!"

Jason was confused, and as the weeks turned to months, he became increasingly agitated. He knew he loved Janice but he also knew that it didn't matter, and he'd do what had to be done. What choice?

"My God, man. I treat people for this crap and I'm about to lose it! Again!" And he knew exactly what that meant. So he made another trip to the bank. The last one. He cleaned out its contents completely. He wouldn't be needing those documents anymore. As for the cross? That was obvious.

This would be the exclamation mark that would conclude this chapter of his life! After this, he vowed to himself and God, he would kill himself before taking another life. But that was later, not now. And he was on a mission.

It no longer mattered who the victim was. It just had to be done and time was of the essence. Why he had ever thought he could lead a normal life was beyond him.

Yet he and Janice had just had the best time of their married life. They had completed a hike through some of the most beautiful scenery he had ever seen. It was no walk in the park but they had conquered it together. And the night on the beach was like no other one before. They were more in love now than they had been throughout their entire marriage.

Jason knew that Janice had been struggling with their relationship, not because it was bad, but that it had become increasingly stale. He knew it as well, and felt that an early exit from the marriage might save her life. He knew he was beginning to lose control. Suddenly the fixation on his "mother" was taking on other dimensions and his desire for satiation was not about to be limited by his "mommy" boundaries. The irony of it was that he really did love her. How was this possible? And how in hell would he ever get into heaven?

He first saw her as she exited the limo at Macy's on Pine Street. My God, was she beautiful! And on impulse, he followed her into the store. Any thought of being discreet had long since vanished. This from the person who thought himself smarter than the rest!

She was obviously well known to the staff, if the way they catered to her was any indication, and money appeared to be no object. My God, she bought more in ten minutes than Janice bought in a year!

And that's when he absently reached for the cross hidden in his breast pocked. That snapped him back to the present and the situation at hand. He wanted her! She was the one! And he wanted her now!

It was late afternoon and shoppers were streaming everywhere. He began to panic. He needed her now! Any thoughts of being discreet were long since gone. He was becoming erratic and beginning to draw attention.

"I've got to get out of here!" under his breath, and finally he was able to steady himself long enough to walk out the door. The fresh air slapped him in the face and the street bench welcomed him come. He collapsed on it as if distressed, and a couple rushed up to him to ensure he was okay. After a few minutes, he was able to escape the glare and made his way back to his vehicle parked a mere block away.

Never had this happened to him before! What had come over him? And still he knew what must be done. Was she still in the store? And what if she was? What now?

And then he saw her. Just down the street. Oh my God! And she was coming his way! Thank you God! So he watched and waited. She passed by his vehicle and slowly made her way to the corner, and then, as if on command, she spun around and headed for the park adjacent to where he was parked.

There was no time to think. The window was open now but it was closing rapidly. Act now or forget it. And that's when he sprung into action.

He surveyed the area as best he could, and then he made his move. She never saw him coming but it wouldn't have mattered anyway. She was his and today she would die! He'd perfected his art to that of a science, and with a quick flick of the wrists it was all over. He glanced around, spotted no one, and gently brought her to the ground.

How he wished he could stay with her a while but he could not. He quickly wrapped the final cross around her hands, asked God to take her home, and that's when he noticed the handbag strewn open. "Make this look like a robbery. Hurry!" To himself. He discreetly made his way back to his vehicle. Then he went back to his office. The sofa reserved for his patients would provide comfort for his sickest patient the rest of that day and well into the night.

Jason may have thought he'd got away with it yet again. But what he didn't realize was that he had just taken down the owner of a high end escort service. She had lots of friends and even more enemies in very high places. This was not over by a long shot!

Janice tried to reach him but to no avail. That was so unlike Jason. But, she had a meeting that evening anyway, so they'd talk later.

When she returned home late that evening, Jason was already asleep. Oh well, we'll talk tomorrow. Perhaps he wasn't feeling well.

JOLINE SEES A PHOTO

Joline settled back into her final semester. She had already received several offers from potential employers and she enjoyed that rare luxury of having a choice, quite an accomplishment in today's competitive market place. But, she was in no rush. In fact, she was seriously contemplating striking out on her own.

She had started a blog the same day she began her university studies and it had found an audience. As her confidence grew, her writing, and I might add, photography, matured to a level where she was beginning to make a decent living off of it. That's when she began to dream really big dreams. Indeed, the world had become her oyster and she'd have the benefit of "no boss!" And she could get on airplanes anytime she liked. The absolute beauty of technology, a prison to some, the gateway to freedom for others! She was one of the "others."

But the reality was that it meant that she spent an inordinate amount of time researching articles, flipping through magazines, listening to endless online podcasts, other blogs, and so on.

But today she was feeling a wee bit homesick and nostalgic. And when that happens she heads to her happy place. Her photo albums, online and otherwise were always there to transport her down memory line. She could, and often did, get lost for hours at a time. Today would be no exception.

Joline couldn't put her finger on it but something was really beginning to bug her. Something about the photos. What was it? This is weird. In any case, she'd wasted quite enough time so back to work. She still had a blog that needed attention and an assignment was due in the next couple of days.

As she worked her mind kept drifting back to the photos. She shrugged it off as best she could until finally she threw her hand up in disgust. "This is ridiculous!" Time for a run! When all else failed there was nothing like a nice long jog to settle her down.

"That feels better." to herself, and she settled into a pace that would push her just hard enough to keep her occupied on the task at hand. Five miles later and she was feeling like the old Joline again. A couple more miles should do it. And it did. A few minutes in the steam room, then drop by the market to pick up a few items, and then home. Finish up the blog and call it day. "Heck, I might even watch some TV for a change."

And that should have been that. But that nagging feeling refused to be put to bed. By now, Joline knew there was more to this than met the eye. Her so called "gut" feeling had baled her out of more than a few situations in the past, and it was definitely acting up! "OK, fine! What's up?" to no one. She often talked to herself, but she'd learned to make sure no one was around when she was having one of "those" conversations.

It was obvious nothing else was going to get done this day so I might as well try and figure this out. So she dug out the photos once again. Methodically. She tried to remember exactly when that feeling had come over her. She hadn't paid any attention to it at the onset because, well, there was no reason to. My God, she must have looked at ten thousand photos, perhaps more. When she took photos, she took photos! And of course, she'd only edited perhaps at most, a thousand of those. Might as well start with those I guess.

Two hours later and nothing! "This is crazy!" But Joline was not one to give up. Hundreds, then thousands more would be scrutinized and then rejected, and soon it was three am. Now she was tired, her eyes were shot, and thankfully she was alone. She would not have made great company right about then.

"That's it! I'm going to bed!" And she did, but it would be a sleepless night. And then, and this is not unusual, she awoke with a start. And a picture in her mind. "Oh my God!"

And now she knew what she was looking for. "Please be wrong! Please be wrong!" she muttered over and over. "Please, please . . ." And there they were. A handful of grab shots that she hadn't done anything with. Snap shots taken, well frankly, just because they were there and she happened to have her camera with her.

She enlarged the images in question on the screen, and then sat back and stared. For a very long time. Finally, she hit "print" and watched three separate images emerge from the portable printer. And then she dug out the article that had sent her on this frenzied path. And sure enough. They were one and the same, at least as far as she could tell. Then she headed to the bathroom. And she puked.

She missed classes the next morning. By that afternoon she was composed enough to send a package anonymously to the lead investigator on the case featured in the aforementioned article.

Now she'd have some decisions to make and she had no idea where to begin.

DEREK RECEIVES A PACKAGE

E very case Derek had ever worked on, cold case and otherwise, was ultimately broken when someone stepped forward, either in person or anonymously, with a tip. Usually it amounted to nothing. But eventually there would be something, something that had either been ignored by the investigators, or just hadn't been credible enough to check out at the time. But with "new" eyes on the job, often the "unseen" became "seen" and what was once dead, was brought back to life.

It wasn't hard to become cynical in this line of work. And there was never enough help or resources, and fresh cases that had a far better chance of being solved would always be the priority. Derek understood this well but it certainly didn't make his job any easier. But on occasion, he'd catch a break. Like what was about to happen now.

"Hey Boss, there's a package for you at the front desk."

"For me?"

"If you're the lead investigator on the Latino serial murder case, then yeah. That's how it's addressed."

Now he was curious. Addressed in block letters:

 Lead investigator

Latino Serial Killer Case

Seattle Division

He'd received parcels before, and all sorts of cryptic messages purporting to know this or that, and most turned out to be bogus. He dares not get his hopes up; not yet. He took the package back to his office and slipped on the spandex gloves so no further evidence might be destroyed. Who knows? "Anonymous" might just know a whole lot more that he was willing to reveal. Perhaps he had inadvertently left a finger print. It's rather handy knowing who one's dealing with.

He unwrapped the package ever so slowly. There were three prints of an individual. There was an article torn from a newspaper that had run a story on this particular case. And there was a name of the fellow in the photos. And in every photo the cross adorning the individual was circled in red.

And there was a note. "Giving this to you will expose me. I'm sure you are quite competent at your job. It's paramount that we speak privately before you talk to this individual. Call me at (xxx) xxx xxxx.

He did. Immediately. She answered and they arranged to meet later that afternoon. Could this be the break? Finally?

She was younger than he had expected. And incredibly attractive, not that that made any difference. Just an observation. She found him to be much as she had expected, perhaps nicer than she was anticipating. She could only imagine what his eyes must see on a daily basis. But it was time to get down to business.

She told him everything she could remember. Right from first meeting him, about her "gut" feelings, and how she'd put it to rest as her Mom seemed perfectly happy. And yet, as she recalled, she had always felt that her Mom was hiding something from her. But when she saw the article about the case something had registered with her and she couldn't figure out what it was. In fact, she barely remembered the article because that's not the type of articles she usually read. And then when she took her trip down memory lane, something registered. It drove her nuts! She couldn't figure out why. But then she remembered the article. She spared him no details.

"But this will kill my Mom. Promise me you'll leave me out of this. I need you to promise."

Here she was, so mature, and yet still a child. He promised her he wouldn't tell her mommy. He didn't actually say that but he did give her his word. And he was a man of his word. They exchanged numbers. He promised to keep her in the loop. She believed him and they went their separate ways. But, it wouldn't be long until they were sharing coffee once again.

YOUR MOM NEEDS YOU

"Your Mom needs you!" Four simple words in a text from an unknown number. Instant panic. Within moments Joline was on the phone. No answer! Cell phone. Nothing! Grandma and Grandpa. Nothing! Texts back to the unknown texter. "Where's my Mom?" No response.

What do I do? Joline was beside herself. Her Mom always answered her call or text immediately. Now there was nothing but silence. Instant decision. "When's your next flight leave for Seattle?" And then "we have one seat available for the flight leaving at 10:30, otherwise we have a flight leaving at 1:00."

"I'll take it, the 10:30." And she proceeded to give the operator her information. "Let's see. It's 8:30 already. Joline always had an emergency bag ready to go. 10 minutes later and she was on her way to the airport. A quick call to her boss and she was cleared for takeoff. Every call/text she attempted was futile. She tried not to panic anymore than she already was, but this was not like her Mom. God, if her Mom tried to call or text her and couldn't get through, she freaked out. Joline was fast approaching freak out status as well!

Where does one's imagination go when one is stressed? Always to the bad stuff, of course. And she couldn't even reach her grandparents. Maybe something had happened to one of them and her Mom was with them at the hospital? And of course, knowing her Mom, she wouldn't want to worry Joline so she wouldn't have called her until she knew for sure what was wrong. Or maybe it was to do with Jason! Please God, not that!

For a brief second she had forgotten about the text. She flipped back to it "Your Mom needs you." Instant goose bumps, and she shivered involuntarily. "Please God, protect my Mom." Joline had been raised as a Christian, and she was a believer, but it seemed like the only time she chatted with God was to ask for something. And here she was again.

And of course she couldn't call during the flight, and she certainly couldn't concentrate on anything else. "Joline" to herself. "Relax. Breathe. It's all going to be fine."

But she wasn't so sure about that. Why would someone test her and not even reveal who they were? A sense of foreboding came over she could not shake. Could this have to do with the photos? She, the calm, cool one was calm no more. And finally, they arrived. Patience, patience. Of course, being stuck at the back of the plane is excruciating even at the best of times, and the line moved as if a bunch of zombies. Patience, relax, patience. Finally!

Still no answer anywhere. She was sure she was pushing the cab driver to break every law there was, but she needed to get to her Moms place now! Oh my God! She had completely forgot to phone Jason! But then how could she? She'd just implicated him in who knows what.

It was as if they had all disappeared. Finally here! She handed the cabbie a 20, no change, thanks, and she bound up the steps to the front door. No use ringing the bell, as she reached for her keys. Thank God her Mom had insisted on her keeping a set, in case of emergency, you never know!

As she scrambled to get the key into the lock the door suddenly opened and she came face to face with . . . she didn't know.

"Who are you? Where's my Mom? I want to see my Mom now!" This was getting weird real fast!

"Joline, come in. I'm Claire, your aunt." And with that, she turned on her heels and beckoned for Joline to follow.

Which she did, silently. Not another word exchanged until they had both sat down. "Alright, what the hell's going on? Is my Mom okay?" Joline could feel the tears welling up in her eyes. "Tell me, please!"

"Your Mom, and your grandparents are fine." Joline sank back into the sofa, and gently began to cry. Tears of relief, but then Claire continued. "Your Mom and grandparents have been taken to a secure location. I'm sorry for the obscure text but I knew it would get you here as quickly as possible. I'll take you to them now."

"What are you telling me? Secure location? My whole family? What about Jason? You never mentioned Jason." And suddenly she was feeling ill. "Tell me now! I have a right to know!"

"Yes you do. Jason was arrested a few hours ago."

"What? Is my Mom . . . Arrested for what?"

"Murder."

"Did you just say murder?"

"Yes, 6 murders."

"I knew it!"

"That's why I'm here. I'll tell you everything later. Right now all you need to know is that your family is fine. I'll explain. Please try and relax. Your Mom is going to need you but I needed to talk to you to explain a few things first."

"Does my Mom even know you're here? She told me that you abandoned us! Why are you here?" This was crazy!

"Okay, let's go. I'll explain as much as I can on the drive over. We've got to get out of here before they see us."

"What? Before who sees us?"

"The press. Let's go, not that way, out the back. I parked down the back alley." Straight out a spy novel, an old one at that. All Joline could do was shake her head. "This is crazy!"

"Okay, heads up. When I say "move," you move. NOW!" And with that they slipped out the back gate, jogged a block down to the waiting vehicle, and sped away. Claire kept checking the rear view mirror and finally, after several blocks, she breathed a sign of relief and proceeded to tell Joline the rest of the story.

Joline felt as though she were in a nightmare and she was unable to wake up. On and on, Claire spun her tale, but alas, this was no tale, and Joline was thrust back into a reality she could not have envisioned. And in a few minutes from now, she'd be face to face with her Mom and grandparents. With everything Claire had just told her, she could not begin to imagine what the three of them must be going through, especially her Mom!

"We'll be there in about ten minutes. Do you want to stop for a few minutes to compose yourself? Your Mom is having a really tough time. You're going to have to be stronger than you've ever been. I know you can do it! I know you better than you think!"

"Okay, pull over for a few minutes. Let me make sure I have this straight. We're hiding from the press right now, right?"

"Yes."

"And my Mom knows you're with me right now?"

"No. She's heavily medicated at the moment. That's why I'm trying to prepare you. Her whole world has just collapsed around her. She kept calling your name. That's when she collapsed and I knew I had to get you here right away. She's fine. She's stabilized. But, I need you to be as calm as possible. You're it. I'm not leaving either of you, ever again."

Joline couldn't wrap her head around Claire. Where did she even come from? No matter. She was here and she was helping her Mom. And her grandparents. We'll deal with the other stuff later.

And then it was time. As soon as her grandparents saw her they rushed to hug her. Not a word was spoken, for what seemed like an eternity, and then her grandma whispered to her "your Mom needs you, but honey, she's not doing well, steel yourself." And she led Joline to the bedroom door.

Joline gently tapped on the door, then entered, "Mom," softly. "It's me, Mom."

Not a word, and then she heard a faint whisper " Joline?"

"It's me, Mom." and Joline joined her Mom on the bed. Not a word was spoken as she drew her Mom as close to her as she could, just like her Mom used to do to her when she was a child, when she had bad dreams, or a cold, or just needed some loving. Roles were reversed but that was okay, because now her Mom needed her.

They lay like that for an hour, neither speaking. Janice trembled as she sobbed and Joline would pull her ever closer. She felt her Mom's forehead for any signs of a fever, and she encouraged her Mom to take a few sips of water.

She had never seen her Mom like this, never even imagined such a scenario, and yet here she was. Finally, she heard her Mom's breathing regulate and her gentle snoring signalled Joline's return to the living room to join the others.

All eyes were upon her as she gently pulled shut the bedroom door. "She's asleep."

They all expected her to say something but there was nothing to say. "We didn't talk. I held her until she fell asleep."

"She didn't say anything?" Gramps.

"Nothing. She cried; she took a few sips of water. That was it."

"Grammy, Gramps, are you okay? I'm so sorry I wasn't here earlier!"

"We're fine. But we were really worried about your Mom. And you."

"Me?"

"We were so scared that some reporter would find you before we could talk to you. That's when Claire decided that the best way was to contact you was the way she did. She knew you'd probably be freaked out but that you'd make your way here the fastest way you could. She was right."

To Claire. "Couldn't you just have called me? At least I would have known what was going on."

I thought about that. But we had the situation well in hand by that time, and I knew your family was safe. That was the most important thing. If you hadn't left a message on your Mom's phone that you were on your way, I would've called you again. As soon as we knew you were on your way, we knew no one would catch up to you before we did."

"Are you some kind of spy or something? I thought you were dead. I'm confused. Why are you here now?"

"Okay, stop. I owe you an explanation. I owe all of you so much more than you'll ever know. And I will explain everything. And if you don't ever want to see me again after this, I'll understand."

Granny and Gramps chimed in "you're not going anywhere! We lost you once, we're not losing you again! End of story!"

But of course it wasn't. There would be many discussions over the coming days. There would be anger. There would be tears, both of joy and sorrow. Claire's past would be revealed in such a way that it would bring them all to tears. And she would speak of her brother, and of her mother, and . . .

But now it was time to speak of Jason. She would speak to them as a reporter. Facts, figures. I need to do it this way so you understand what has happened here. I need to stay dispassionate for the moment. I need to tell you everything I know right now, and also tell you what to expect over the coming months. Nothing I have to say is easy, and you'll have the spotlights of the world on you. You are going to have to pull together like never before. Fortunately, you are a close family, and you're strong. You'll need to be. And if you'll allow me, I'll be here every step of the way!" Claire took a deep breath, and was about to continue when the bedroom door opened. Janice stood there staring at them and then, as if in slow motion, slowly slipped to the floor. Claire rushed to her side, and they gently helped her to the couch. Janice tried to speak but the words were unintelligible. "Grab a pillow and a blanket." They made her as comfortable as they could but it was obvious that simple medicine was not going to mend a very broken heart!

JANICE IS BACK

It seems the best medicine is always the simplest. They fed Janice a steady diet of her mom's chicken soup, her favourite tea, and a whole bunch of loving. Her parents slipped into the next room to pray since Janice was anything but open to this God who would let this happen to her. How dare He? She had served him her entire life and He let her marry a serial killer? If that's what God was all about, then they were done!

Janice had never questioned her Christianity before. She never really had to. Her life had always been good, even when she'd gotten pregnant out of wedlock, her parents, as well as her church, were there for her the entire time. It wasn't easy, but she remembered thanking God for all the blessings in her life, and especially for the birth of her little girl, Joline. But that was then.

A loving God would not have let her marry a serial killer! My God, she had pursued Jason until he finally got it and asked her to marry him! What did that make her?

Thoughts after thoughts exploded in her fragile mind. That last night of their honeymoon when he'd acted so weird came rushing back. Those other times when she'd sensed something but couldn't put her finger on it. His "too perfect" everything.

The perfect husband, the perfect dresser, the perfect organizer, and so on. Even their wonderful trip to La Push and the unforgettable night spent on the beach was called into question. How many times had he thought about killing me? And she would collapse exhausted yet again, and again, and again.

There would be no relief for Janice these days. But she was a fighter, and she would confront this monster called Jason. She needed to face him. And it would be soon!

Her parents, Joline, and Claire would spend countless hours in consultation with the private nurse they had hired to monitor Janice. All agreed that her condition was fragile, at best. If this went on much longer, she would need to be hospitalized.

Especially concerning was Janice's insistence that she see Jason. It was going to happen one way or the other. They knew it, and either they would help her or she'd do it on her own. What choice did they have? Obvious answer. So they stepped up.

Janice knew how scared her family was for her. She, the strong, determined one, reduced to a pile of mush. But never had she been faced with such pain! She had trusted him fully. When she committed she was all in, body, mind, and soul. And she had brought her parents along for the ride. They loved Jason! Had, anyway. And he'd betrayed them all. He'd killed people! My God!

God! I thought you were real. What a joke! And she began to sob once again. I can't believe this is happening! Why, God, why? And once again she had to catch herself. She'd been ingrained believing in God her entire life, and now she didn't know what to believe. How could a loving God allow this to happen? In fact, how could he allow all the terrible things going on in the world to happen?

And then, on the fifth day of her isolation, she awoke, slipped into the bathroom, and proceeded to ready herself for the day's events. Everyone else was still sleeping so she slipped into the kitchen for a long overdue cup of coffee. She perched on the stool at the end of the island and slowly began to unravel the events of the past few days.

And that's when her Dad joined her. She didn't notice him at first. He'd been up for the better part of an hour already, settled into the lazy boy just off the kitchen. He'd always risen early. He called this his God time. This was his time to really listen to God; he'd built it up to over half an hour every morning. Then it'd be his turn to ask God for whatever was on his heart. Right now, he and God were spending all sorts of time praying for Janice. Father, cover her with the blood of Jesus! And of course, he always had time for all the significant people in his life, and whoever else he could squeeze in before the events of the day forced their way into his thoughts.

He'd heard her rise, and in fact, darn near asked her to make him a coffee, but he thought better of it. He'd continue what he was doing while keeping an eye on her. She was a strong girl, this one. He knew that at some point, she'd gather herself together, and when that happened, he wanted to be close by. And now was the time.

"Hon." And Janice jumped. "Sorry, I didn't mean to startle you." Her Dad, ever the gentleman.

"Hi pops, did I wake you?" She knew the answer; he'd been doing this for as long as she could remember.

"No, I was up. That coffee sure smells good!"

"I'll make you one." She'd done this more than a time or two over the years.

"Dad, I'm sorry that I scared you so much, all of you. I lost it. I completely lost it Dad. I've never felt so broken, ever. I thought I was going to die!"

"I know honey. You had us pretty scared there for awhile. Thank God Claire was here. And that daughter of yours, wow, you raised her right, I can tell you that!"

"Dad, I don't understand," and as composed as she was trying to be, he could see her trembling as the tears gently made their way down her cheeks onto the tip of her chin. He quickly rose and held his baby girl as tightly as he could. "I know, baby, I know. None of us do."

"I have to see Jason."

"I know you do. I've talked to everyone here. I told them that we'd know when you're ready. And not to try and talk you out of it. They understand."

He continued "Claire has been in contact with the authorities so they are aware that you'll be requesting a meeting fairly soon. Jason also requested a meeting with you. In fact, he won't talk to anyone else until he talks to you, apparently. Would I love to get my hands on him!" She'd never heard her Dad even raise his voice, let along talk like that!

She, on the other hand, actually, she didn't know what she'd do. This wasn't her world. My God, everything she'd ever written was about the good in people, not the bad! I mean, she'd alluded to it obviously, but good always triumphed evil in all of her novels, and especially in her children's series.

How would anyone ever take her seriously again? She, the award winning, best selling author who wrote about everyone else, was the wife of a serial killer. And she didn't know? Give me a break! She had to know something was off! Come on! Do you think we're stupid or something?

Because, that's how she thought. How was it possible that she didn't know at least something? She'd asked herself that a thousand times these past four days. And no answer was forthcoming.

By this time the rest of the gang was stirring to life. Seeing Janice sitting there composed, brought them all back to life in quick order. "Hey Mom". And there was her baby girl just waiting for her turn to hug her. "Mommy, I was so scared." And then there was Claire. They studied each other awkwardly, and then Janice slipped off her stool, approached Claire and hugged her, and they both began to cry. Both of their bodies shook from the uncontrollable sobbing and that's when the rest of them joined in. For the longest time, not a word was spoken, and then as if on command, they all began talking at once. And that's when it happened. Janice began to giggle, then Claire, then Joline, and soon they were all laughing so hard that one could have sworn there was a party going on! But this was a party that no one here wanted to attend!

JANICE VISITS JASON
IN JAIL

So Claire made the call. They were expecting it and plans were made to meet that very afternoon. It would just be the two of them. Both were allowed to have a lawyer present but that was it. Both declined the offer.

Janice was back. Her parents and Joline knew it. Claire was beginning to get it. And Jason? He already knew how formidable she was. Frankly, he was intimidated, but he had to talk to her. He had to try and explain the inexplainable.

She'll understand. I know she will. I know she still loves me. She knows I'd never hurt her! Oh God, thank you! Thank you!

Jason was beside himself. She wouldn't come if she didn't still love me. See! I knew it. He needed to prepare. "Guard, I need to shave! My wife is coming to see me!"

He couldn't believe how nervous he was! "I guess that's what being in love does to a person." to himself. "Oh happy day!"

The abyss had called his name and he had succumbed to it willingly. He didn't know that at the time but it became readily apparent to those who knew him. He hadn't been an easy person to get to know, and although respected for his extraordinary mind, he had always walked on the other side of the street. They had tried to include him on numerous occasions but his overt arrogance put the others off to such a degree that they forged ahead without him. Being around him felt like one was being put under the lens of a microscope. For Gods sake man, this is a social gathering! Better not to invite him. Stay on the other side of the street for all we care!

And then it was time. "Oh my God, she's here!" to the guard. "I can't wait to see her!" He shook his head. "These crazies are all the same." he muttered under his breath.

So they explained the rules, and marched him to the waiting room. He was locked down as per regulations. God he was nervous! He kept slicking back his hair. "Oh my God, here she comes."

It's time. The rules of engagement were explained to both of them. Any violation of said agreement and the interview is over. Got it?

Jason was marched out first. Orange jump suit. Leg shackles. Hand cuffs. Sit down at the table. Prisoner secured to the floor. Guard in room at full alert.

Janice took a deep breath, walked in and sat down, never taking her eyes off Jason. He held her gaze until she was fully settled. Janice was as composed as as a cucumber. Jason was unnerved. This was not going to go well.

Finally Jason spoke, fumbling for words. She involuntarily sneered at his inadequacy. Mr. Big Man. Not so big anymore, are you?

"I never meant for this to happen. I need you to believe me. I would never harm you." Janice remained silent. He continued

"I know you'll find this hard to believe but I love you, I've always loved you!" Again, she didn't speak, unnerving Jason even further. "Please say something."

She sat there looking at this pathetic creature she had called her husband only days before. Then she spoke "Who are you? Who the hell are you?" He was taken aback by her tone. She had never spoken to him like this. Never! And that's when he knew that it mattered not what he said. He was dead to her. Dead! Dead and buried!

And that's when he began to cry "Please talk to me. I need you to talk to me. Please!" This intellectual who was so much smarter than anyone else was made the more pathetic by his blubbering.

And all she felt was contempt for this excuse for a human being. And that's when she began to talk. "Don't you dare say a word until I'm finished talking!" Oh what a reversal of roles! And he didn't say another word.

She continued "You killed at least 6 women. 6! Are there more? Tell me right now or I'm leaving!" She was definitely in control! "I want to know now!"

And before he knew it, Jason was telling her everything, and the cameras they had fixed on them right from the start. Derek, as well as Claire who was allowed to join him, gasped at what they were hearing.

Detail after details rolled off Jason's lips. My God, he'd even murdered his parents! And he didn't stop talking. The interview was supposed to last an hour. They waived that rule and prayed he'd go on. Janice hadn't moved a bit and they prayed she'd hang in there. She wasn't going anywhere, and with each breath Jason took them deeper and deeper into his world. Not one did he request a lawyer. And he talked and he talked as if there were no tomorrow. Perhaps he knew something they didn't. Janice never budged, and if at any point Jason appeared to be wrapping it up, she'd ask another leading question. This went on for over two hours. And as abruptly as he had started talking he stopped. "I have nothing more to say!"

When he stopped, Janice got up, never said a word, and walked out of the room. Jason began to scream "You promised me you'd talk to me. I need to talk to you. I need to tell you something. It's important. I love you! Please, please don't go. Its not fair. How can you do this to me? After everything I've done for you! Come back! Please!" But she didn't. And that's when he began to scream. And that's when the guards dragged him back to his cell. And that's when he realized how much he'd said to her and to the watching cameras.

They sedated him and placed him on suicide watch. This guy was seriously crazy, by anyone's measure! And he was a Doctor! My God, how could you ever send anyone to someone like him?

Had they seen him out in the so called real world, they would have bowed down to him like all the other peasants, at least that's what Jason thought! Cretins!

Janice had never been so scared in all her life! She had seen evil personified. She had watched evil speak. She wanted to puke. But he was talking and every word was another nail in his coffin. So she stayed. If she could have spoken she may have said something. She couldn't but thank God he didn't know that. And now he had hung himself!

She didn't know what to feel. They had been together over four years. No way! Not with that person in the other room.

There was no way that could have happened. And yet it did. My God! God, I'll give you one more chance to explain yourself! Yeah, right!

When Janice emerged, she was met immediately by Claire. This was not the Janice that had met with Jason. This Janice could barely breathe and if not for Claire rushing to her aid, she would have surely collapsed. She was spent completely. She needed to sleep. Now. Claire gently rocked her as she stroked her hair. "Now, now, it's ok, baby girl." And that's how Derek met Janice. And that's when he knew he'd never let go of Claire. Ever!

"She needs to rest. Let's take her back to the hotel. I'll call ahead so they know we're on our way."

Derek went to get Claire's car. He'd get one of the guys to take his vehicle back to headquarters. He needed to be with Claire and Janice right now. It was time to meet the rest of the family.

He could barely contain the excitement within. My God, Janice had gotten Jason to reveal more information than they could have gotten from him in a lifetime. It was like he needed to be exorcised. By her. And man, what a job she'd done! "I bet she has no idea of what she's done!" to himself.

And of course, she didn't know. And she'd be no further help for the next couple of days. Upon their arrival she was immediately whisked to bed, without protest. And that's when Claire could final introduce Derek to her family. "Derek I want you to meet", and hesitating ever so slightly, "my Mom and my Dad." Tears were streaking down Claire's face as she spoke, as they were on not only her parents, but on Joline's face as well.

"Young man," Dad was always in control " Welcome to our family!"

Derek had never had this kind of love, even with his parents. And here they were, inviting him in just like he'd always belonged. Claire had told him about these people and how scared she'd been when she knocked on Janice's door just a few days ago, and about how her parents had embraced her like the prodigal son, okay, daughter, and how accepted she had felt immediately. And watching her now, and the way they interacted, all of them, and seeing Claire and Janice's bond at the jail was overwhelming. And what Janice had just pulled off? Oh my God!

She might have pulled it off but it wasn't because she was in control. In fact, it was the opposite. She was totally freaked out. Thank God Jason had kept talking! And did he spill the beans! What shocked her the most was that it didn't matter what he said any more. They had lived a lie and now each of them would have to live with the consequences. At least he was in jail. Her jail was much larger.

But she would rise to the occasion. Just a few days ago she would have rather died than deal with the fallout that she knew was coming. How could she blame anyone for doubting her? After all, how couldn't she have suspected something? There had to be signs, surely to God?

These were the same questions, and a hundred more, that she asked herself ad nauseum. But the answers were always the same. I didn't know. Having her family gather around her the way they had was priceless. And then there was Claire. Where do I even start? Where would I be if Claire hadn't shown up? I don't know if I would have survived. And Mom and Dad welcomed her just like she'd never left. So many questions!

And my beautiful, precious daughter! She rushed home the moment she knew I was in trouble. And now she and Claire were inseparable! What a crazy world!

JOLINE TELLS JANICE ABOUT THE PHOTOS

Joline knew she'd have to tell her Mom the whole story, and she'd have to do it soon. It was only fair. She knew it would cut her Mom like a knife. Because that's when the "if only" would begin in earnest. If only I would have done this or that, lives could have been saved. It's my fault. If only . . . She was going to have to handle this carefully. Perhaps Claire should be there when this goes down.

This whole thing was surreal. Had she not found those photos, she would have never met Derek. And if she hadn't met Derek, Claire never would have shown up at her Mom's door. And now, a family divided was a family reunited. How does one even begin to explain this? Coincidence? I don't think so!

"Mom, we need to talk. You, me, and Claire. Just the three of us. OK?"

"Of course, hon. Why Claire?"

"Trust me, Mom. It's important."

So they set it up. They didn't want to do it in front of the others, but they weren't sure if meeting in public was wise either. What if Janice lost it? That wasn't likely but there was nothing normal about any of this. But they worked it out and travelled together to the venue. Any attempt at small talk was futile, and the radio mercifully filled the void.

Janice wasn't sure what to think about this. Why didn't they just tell her what they had to say? And why did Joline insist on having Claire join them? Jeez, how'd they get so close? I'm starting to get peed off. And they finally arrived. Janice was the first out of the vehicle. "Come on, hurry up!"

"Oh, oh, Mom's losing it." she whispered to Claire.

And indeed she was. They were finally seated, but Janice was having no more of this cat and mouse game. "Spit it out! Now!"

And spit they did! "Mom, do you remember when I told you that I thought something was wrong and you blamed it on your tour schedule? That was a long time ago but I knew in my gut that something wasn't right. Do you remember that?"

"Of course, hon, but I was freaked out over the tour. That's the truth!"

" I knew you were but there was more to it than that. I just knew it!"

"I did to. But I didn't know what and I didn't want you to worry about me. It's not like you didn't have enough on your plate already!"

"But then I kind of forgot about it; figured my imagination was acting up as usual, and if there was anything really wrong, that you'd tell me. And you never did, so I kinda forgot about it."

Janice decided that she might as well tell them everything. Right down to Jason's strange behaviour on their honeymoon. "It's weird talking to you like this."

"I know Mom, but it's important."

"Ok, well that really floored me but Jason really opened up then, and I decided to just let it go. I admit, I started watching a little closer after that, but he was so loving. He'd do anything for me, and I finally just forgot about it. Well, maybe not forgot about it exactly, but I quit holding it against him. We all have our hang ups and he'd had a terrible life growing up. Anyway, that's what happened."

Joline continued "Mom, I know you're wondering about Claire but please bear with me. You need to hear this. From me. I only came up a couple of times over the next couple of years, but I knew in my heart that something was just not right. I couldn't put my finger on it, and you seemed so happy and I didn't want to jeopardize that. So I left it. But Mom, every time I came home it always felt too perfect. That's what freaked me out. He was always really nice, but I just got bad vibes when I was around him."

"Hon, why didn't you say something to me? You know you can tell me anything!"

"I know Mom, but this was different!"

Joline wanted to talk. Janice bit her lip. Claire listened. Her turn would come soon enough. So far, this was going pretty smoothly.

Ok, it was time. "You know how you were always on me about taking pictures."

"I wasn't on you . . ."

"Sorry! I didn't mean anything by that, but you always want me to take pictures, right?"

"Right, and?"

"And I did. Lots every time I was home, especially at your Anniversary."

"So?" Where was this going?

"Well, I was going through my photos one day and something kept bugging me and I couldn't figure out what it was. I must have went through those photos fifty times! I didn't even know why or what I was looking for but I kept going over them, again and again. Finally, I just went to bed. But three or so, boom, I was wide awake and I knew what I was looking for!"

"What?" Janice interrupted.

"This." and Claire slipped the photos in question to Janice.

"I don't understand. What am I missing?"

And that's where Claire took over. Janice was even more confused.

"Just hear me out." and Claire told her about Derek.

"Derek the detective? The guy that I met the other day?"

"Yes. He's the lead detective on the Latino case."

"I'm sorry. I'm missing something here."

Joline butted in. "Mom, When I saw these photos of Jason, I knew that I'd seen that cross that he wears somewhere before. I just knew it! But I couldn't figure out why I knew, or even what the big deal was. And then I remembered where I'd seen that cross before."

On she went " you know I'm always researching everything. Well, I was flipping through a magazine when I saw that cross."

"Jason's cross?"

"Yes! I knew it! So I dug up the article and I printed off those photos I'd taken at your guys place, and sure enough, they were a match! That's when I freaked out! I wanted to call you but I was scared that you'd confront him and he'd kill you!"

Janice got up and headed straight to the bathroom. "Should I go with her?" Claire to Joline. "No, give her a moment."

Within a few minutes she was back. "Go on."

So I decided to send the photos and the article to the lead detective on the case. I gave him my number and asked him to meet me before they confronted Jason. Mom, I was so scared! But I didn't know what else to,do!"

Janice could only shake her head, back and forth she went, head in hands, mumbling to herself. "Oh my God!"

CLAIRE TELLS JANICE EVERYTHING

ow it was Claire's turn. "My official job is Investigative Reporting. I work out of the Houston office but I make my home now in Seattle. Derek is my fiancé and we work together on some of the more interesting cold cases. This was a case that we had already put a serious amount of time into but like all these cases, we needed a break of some sort. And then Derek got a package from some anonymous source claiming knowledge of this particular case. We get lots of these so called leads, but we can't afford to ignore any of them. When Derek opened up the package it contained the newspaper article that Joline had mentioned, as well as these photos, and the name of the individual in the photos. Also, a phone number of the sender which he called immediately. And that's really where I come in." Claire paused.

Joline jumped in "Mom, I knew it was him the moment I saw that cross! I was so scared but I knew I had to do something."

Claire continued "When Derek told me about the package, and when we began looking into Jason, well naturally, your name came up, and I knew I had no choice. Part of the reason I was back in Seattle was to try and make amends to a family that I had treated so cruelly. I needed to try and explain why I had left. They deserved way more than that but I was chicken and I knew they must hate me! But when your name came up, well, that was it! I was in and the time was now! And that was my baby sister, and . . ." Claire began to cry. And that's when Janice wrapped her arms around her, and rocked her back and forth. Little sister comforting big sister while Joline looked on.

And finally Claire was able to continue "I had done a lot of research on crosses and just wasn't getting anywhere. All the crosses were exactly the same so we figured there had to be some significance but we kept drawing a blank. But when that package arrived we finally had something. We had been pretty accurate on our timeline but still no closer to the identify of the perpetrator. Now we had a name. So we did the research into Jason, and of course into you as well. What choice did I have after that?"

Janice was stunned. She kept nodding her head but this lady of words had none. Finally "Can we go home now? Please. I need to sleep."

And that's where it ended for now.

JASON AFTER JANICE'S CONFRONTATION

Jason was screwed and he knew it! How dare she throw him to the wolves! Besides, she was his wife. She couldn't legally testify against her husband. Or could she? "I want my lawyer now!"

But he talked. The less she said, the more he said. And the cameras picked up every word. For once, being the smartest person in the room simply meant that he was in the room alone. That was it. Smart ass! And for some reason or other, the other prisoners had taken a dislike to him. Imagine that! So he was put into isolation for his own safety. Why they didn't like him he didn't know. "Bunch of low life's!"

The hour a day he was allowed to go into the yard to get some exercise were harrowing for him. Although accompanied by a guard to assure his safety, he could hear their taunts. "You're gonna die. We're coming for you! Better start praying!" and so on. He was safe, wasn't he? Wasn't he?

But if he expected any sympathy from anyone, it wasn't coming. Not even his own lawyer. What did his lawyer say to him? "I don't have to like you. I just have to defend you, and that I'll do. Off the record, I hope you burn! You're nothing but a waste of skin!" And he was the best money could buy! Things were not looking good for Jason!

Jason's concern would all be for naught anyway. They tried to let him have his hour outside when the other prisoners were locked up, less chance of something going awry. It seemed to work quite well and soon Jason was back to being his smart ass self. Guys like him didn't get it. Life is fragile at the best of times. In here, you were one shiv away.

Jason prayed constantly. In his rational moments he knew he was never getting out of this place. But, he also knew God. And God's Word promised him eternal life if he accepted Christ as his Savior. He had done that long ago, and even though he knew he had committed heinous acts, and would do so again if he were let out, he would stand on the Word. So that's what he did.

And it was well that he did, for one night while wandering the courtyard he found himself decidedly not alone. The guard had excused himself "I've got to slip to the can. I'll be right back." It no longer mattered. He felt their presence before he saw them. Screaming was futile. Only a single word was spoken. "Payback!" Jason began to pray earnestly. He was unafraid. Under his breath "I hope it doesn't hurt too much." and then back to his praying.

It hurt. No question about it. But obviously the fellow wielding the shiv knew what he was doing. It entered through his back, and they would determine later that it had pierced his heart. They lowered him to the ground as gently as one might handle a child, and slipped back to wherever they had come from.

When the guard returned he found Jason laying on the ground in a pool of blood. He screamed for help and was soon joined by others. But it was too late.

The guards would later say that Jason had waved them away in his last moments. And, that he was singing. It creeped them out.

When asked what he was singing, the guard whispered softly "Jesus loves me this I know, for the Bible tells me so. Over and over he kept singing that and then, just before he died, he said Father, forgive them . . . that's when I lost it!"

There would be an enquiry. The guard on duty would be reprimanded for abandoning his post. The perpetrators were identified but it didn't matter. They were all serving multiple life sentences already. What was there to threaten them with? Even so, a celebration was held in the prison the following day. Justice had been done according to those on the inside.

When Janice first heard that Jason had been murdered in prison, her heart went out to him. For a moment. But the reality of what he had done far outweighed any sympathy she now felt. What was there to say? Anything out of her mouth would be misinterpreted regardless of how she chose her words. So she remained silent.

JANICE VISITS JASON

No one was more surprised than Janice at how quickly she had regained control of her life. The accusations that she had expected just didn't materialize. It seemed no one was blaming her for anything, not that they should have been, but people can be cruel. She was especially gratified at the outpouring of love she received from her fans.

But there was much more to the story, and it wasn't something she wanted to share with her fans or her family, for that matter. Yes, Jason had done those horrible things. He admitted it. But, he was sick and that should count for something, shouldn't it? He must have felt so terribly alone. Even she had abandoned him! "I wonder what God thought about that?" she mused to herself.

Jason knew God. She was sure of that. Not that she could ever understand how God works all this stuff out. But she kept her thoughts to herself, less they think she was crazy as well.

At night when she was totally alone she could allow her mind to wander. And wander it did, and it usually went to the wonderful, loving side of Jason that no one else knew about. The side that her so called friends were so envious of since their husbands acted like a bunch of neanderthals. Of course, now they were saying something much different. And they were nowhere to be found. Big surprise!

Janice poured herself into her work as most everyone had expected. Her family was thrilled at how well she was doing. What they didn't know was that Janice, in addition to her ongoing projects, was working on something quite different, something they would have found quite disturbing.

This project took on a life of its own and over time it would consume her if she wasn't careful. This was her Project X and it would be written under a pen name unbeknownst to anyone but her. And it would involve Jason, the Jason I knew, not the Jason that the world thinks they knew. Had her family known this they would have whisked her away to a mental hospital in quick order. They were just like everyone else; they just didn't get it!

Had anyone been watching her closely, they may have picked up some signs early on. They may have noticed that she left the house unusually early in the morning, but so what? Probably just going to grab a coffee and have a quiet moment before the day's craziness took over. They would have been right about the coffee. And the quiet time. But they would have freaked out had they known who she was having coffee with.

Had they got close enough to her they may have noticed the tiny cross dangling from her finger tips. And they may have heard her singing, ever so softly, "Jesus loves me, this I know . . . For the Bible tells me so . . . Little ones to Him belong . . . They are weak but He is strong . . ."

EPILOGUE
ONE YEAR LATER

The past year was surreal. Mikey stood just inside the gate that would grant him freedom. He merely had to walk through it. Claire had backed up her promise in spades. She knew the right people, and within months, His case was brought before a review board, and now, a year later, he stood at the door granting him his freedom.

He had fought Claire on this. This place was his life. He was living his God given purpose behind these walls. He was changing or at least contributing towards change in so many of the inmates. Surely this was God's calling on his life. But still, how could he ignore the one thing everyone in this place desired. Freedom. Even though many were unable to handle it once it was given, they still craved it, and he had to admit, so did he. But, he was scared. In here he was safe. He had to laugh at the absurdity of it all. With a final sigh, he stepped through the doorway and into the light. "Please God, help me find my way."

There they stood. Claire and O'Malley, with smiles as big as their hearts! They hugged, they laughed, and they cried. But this time the tears were tears of joy!

These two had left nothing to chance. O'Malley had plenty of room at his place. Mikey could stay with his as long as he liked. Truth is, he was probably more excited about it than Mikey. That old house was pretty darn lonely since his wife had passed.

And Claire? Well, she needed Mikey. She'd already cleared it with Pastor Rick. She and Derek had already set a tentative date; confirmation would depend on Mikey's release date. Tomorrow they would confirm it. Mikey would perform the wedding. Her Dad and Mom would give her away. Janice would be her bridesmaid. O'Malley and her boss would be the best men. And Joline would serve a few roles; that of flower girl, as well as songstress for them as they entered the chapel, and "unofficial" photographer.

Mikey, while indeed honoured at Claire's request, was seriously stressed. He would do as she requested. But it would take every once of jam he could muster. And even though he'd only been out a few days, he'd been getting calls from former inmates wanting to meet. And that would violate his parole.

He knew he'd be tested. And he didn't know if he'd pass. That was the only life he knew, and being out here was scaring the hell out of him! Why didn't Claire and O'Malley just leave things alone? What happens if I blow this?

What Mikey didn't know was that Pastor Rick was already hard at work on his behalf. He had long wanted to get involved in prison ministry but time and money never aligned at the same time. But with Mikey's knowledge of the prison system and of the true needs of the inmates, this may be exactly the right time!

He hadn't even mentioned this to Mikey yet in case it went nowhere. But after getting some positive vibes from the council, Rick decided that he and Mikey needed to talk. The pay would be substandard, which was no big surprise, but the possibilities to make a difference were endless. And that's something Claire had stressed over and over to him. Mikey was fighting getting out of the prison because he believed God was using him exactly where he was.

So Rick made the call. They agreed to meet at the Church. Mikey assumed Rick wanted to go over the details of the big day fast approaching. They made small talk and discussed the upcoming nuptials as expected. But then Rick dropped the bombshell. Mikey was stunned! "Are you saying that I can still work at the prison with the inmates, except that now I'll get paid for it?"

"That's exactly what I'm saying. It's not quite done yet but I had to share this with you. Both of us praying can't hurt! Of course, you won't be living at the prison but I'm confident we can work out something that'll give you as much access as you need. You get to continue your work but there'll be a lot more resources available to you. You in?"

"Am I in? Oh my God! Yes! Thank you God!" Mikey had to tell Claire. He was like a kid! And that felt so good. He had to tell her in person. "Claire, we need to meet. Right now." Claire was instantly alarmed. "Oh my God! What happened?" Funny how we always assume the worst. "No, no, it's all good. Can we meet?" "Ok, I'll be wrapped up in an hour and I'll drop by your place." "Don't be late!" He yelled into the phone before unceremoniously hanging up.

When Claire finally arrived Mikey was practically bouncing off walls! "What's come over you?" "Guess. Come on, just try and guess." Yep, he was definitely a kid again. Wholly crap! " Mikey, spit it out!" And finally, he told her and she pulled a Mikey! Now there were two of them acting like a couple of teenagers. That's when O'Malley walked in. "What the heck of you two been smoking?" They started to giggle and before long, he had joined in. He had no idea what he was giggling about, but it sure felt good!

So they told him. "Thank you God! Mikey, I have to tell you, I was starting to get worried. I knew you were getting some calls, and as much as I hate to say it, the only people you know are either in jail or were in jail, and with your parole on the line, I was having my doubts whether this was going to work out or not. This is fantastic news!"

It was! But it would take time. Mikey was finding life on the outside a whole lot harder than on the inside. And O'Malley wasn't around all the time. But they were, and they weren't letting up!

JANICE AND CLAIRE

Janice and Claire had become inseparable. Years that had been lost were recaptured as best they could be. But they weren't going to stay there. They were here and the time was now. They both marvelled at their parents. Janice knew how heartbroken her parents had been when Claire walked out of their lives. Yet they had never spoken an ill word of her. And then how they'd welcomed her back into their lives without a second thought. But that really shouldn't have surprised them. These two were the very foundation that this family was built upon. They walked their faith day in and day out, and although hell may one day freeze over, this house would stand forever!

Claire would regale Derek with her and Janice's tales of shopping, and lunches, and memories of a time long since past. She giggled as she told him story after story, he patiently taking it all in. He loved seeing her this way! He chuckled as he remembered their first meeting. She was all business back then. All that mattered was "the story." Emotional? Not her! But now? He loved it!

JOLINE MAKES AN ABRUPT CHANGE

The events of the past year had a profound effect on Joline. She was certain that she had her life planned out pretty well. Freelance blogger, travelling the world, getting involved in social causes wherever she felt she could make a difference, and generally just having a great time.

She still was, but the lustre had come off the apple. And like it or not, she missed her family big time! Maybe she'd better rethink this whole thing. Claire reappearing in their lives had really impacted her. Plus watching her Mom and Claire behaving like school girls, made her envious of not having a sibling! And maybe she should look into investigative reporting a little more seriously, after all, it wasn't like she didn't have connections!

AS FOR JANICE

Janice may have had her secrets and her reasons for keeping them thus. But others were watching and listening. And biding their time.

THE END

DD ANDER BIO

DD ANDER never did fit in very well in the prairie town he grew up in. While his classmates were settling down to careers and raising families, he was dreaming of mountain peaks and tall ships. And though he would attempt to follow those dreams, he always ended up back home on the prairies.

For a good part of his life he stayed the course, but eventually, he took his leave. He travelled extensively, and his experiences would soon catch up with his passion for a different life.It would take him into places he should not have trod, and into experiences he should not have had. Stories would be told, by him, that he would deem fiction, but those who knew him, knew not where the fiction ended and the truth began. And they dared not ask.

Duane began to blog regularly during this time. Hundreds of blogs would follow, and to those who knew him well, it became obvious that the greater story lie between the lines. The public story was there for all the world to see, the other, for certain eyes only.

Although he lives in another part of the world today, he is always close by in one form or another. Whether through his blogs, his photos, his novels, both fiction and non-fiction, or his one on one conversations, he is never very far away.